ABU MUSA'S WOMEN NEIGHBORS

Library of Congress Cataloging-in-Publication Data

Toufiq, Ahmed.
⌈Jarat Abi Musá. English⌉
Abu Musa's women neighbors : a historical novel from Morocco / Ahmed
Toufiq ; translated into English by Roger Allen.
p. cm.
ISBN 0-942996-56-9
I. Allen, Roger M. A. II. Title.

PJ7864.A4718J3713 2005
892.7'36—dc22

Originally published as *Jārāt Abi Mūsā* by Dar Al Kubat Al Zarqua` in Marrakech,
Morocco.© Ahmed Toufiq 1997.

© The Post-Apollo Press for the U.S. Edition 2006.

Cover photographs, book design, and typesetting by Hatem Imam.

The Post-Apollo Press
35 Marie Street Sausalito California 94965

Printed in the United States of America on acid-free paper.

ABU MUSA'S WOMEN NEIGHBORS

A historical novel from Morocco

Ahmed Toufiq

Translated from the Arabic by
ROGER ALLEN

THE POST-APOLLO PRESS
Sausalito, California

By the Same Author

Novels:

Al-Sayl, 1998
Gharibat Al-Husayn, 2000
Shujayrat Hinna' Wa-Qamar, 1998
Jarat Abi Musa, 1st ed., 1997; 2nd ed., 2000

Works Edited by Ahmed Toufiq:

Ibn Al-Zayyat Al-Tadili, Al-Tashawwuf Ila Rijal Al-Tasawwuf, 1998
*Muhammad Al-Kili, Mawahib Dhi Al-Jalal Fi Nawazil Al-Bilad
        Al-Sa'ibah Wa-Al-Jibal,* 1998
Al-`azafi, Da`amat Al-Yaqin Fi Za`amat Al-Muttaqin, 1989

ABU MUSA'S WOMEN NEIGHBORS

For Zaynab, Jumanah, and Ghaythah,
For Muhammad Ays, Samir, Jad, and Muhammad Yubas

CHAPTER ONE

Friday prayer-flags were fluttering over the minarets when the messenger rode up to the city of Salé on a black horse. At the Marisah gate guards checked his identity, then allowed him to enter. One of them ran in front and escorted him immediately to the house of the Chief Judge, Ibn al-Hafid. The visitor took a seat on a shady bench in the vestibule of the Judge's riyad.* While he was waiting, two servants inquired about his mission and served him some chilled water and a tray of food. They shared the latest gossip about Salé itself, the things they had heard about events in the Sultan's capital of Fez, and the latest from Tamisna, the region from which the messenger had just arrived.

The Judge returned from Friday prayers and entered the riyad by the family door. Informed that a court messenger was waiting to speak to him, he made his way to the little

---

Riyad: a traditional multi-story house in Moroccan cities, built around a central courtyard.

room by the third vestibule in order to receive his guest.

The messenger greeted him. "My master, the Supreme Judge, Abu Salim al-Jawra'i, counselor to His Majesty the Sultan," he said, "has sent me to inform you that, as part of his return journey from Tamisna to Fez, he and his retinue propose to pay you a visit this evening. He asks you to inform the Governor of Salé and his courtiers, especially men of culture, of his arrival."

Ibn al-Hafid realized what a great honor was being bestowed on him, not merely because of Al-Jawra'i's exalted status but also because the obvious preferment involved would enhance his own prestige at the expense of the Governor, someone for whom only one name was ever used in the privacy of the Judge's own home, "the odious."

Ibn al-Hafid went at once to the quarters of his junior wife, Tumaymah (that is the way he used to familiarize her name, one already reduced by her family to Al-Tam from Tamu, that itself being a contraction of Fatimah). His eldest son by his senior wife, himself a renowned poet and cavalier, had often refrained from suggesting an alternative derivation to his father, for fear of hurting his feelings, namely that Tumaymah could also be a diminutive of Tamah, meaning "disaster."

Tumaymah was well aware that the Judge's request that she be the one to organize a ceremonial banquet for the most important representative of the Sultan to visit the house up till now was an acknowledgment of the skills she had inherited from long-standing tradition in the house of her father who was Judge in Sijilmasah, a city involved in the gold-trade with the Sudan. Auburn-haired and as svelte as a reed-stalk (as they described her), she was endowed with a tough streak that served her well when it came to terrorizing everyone, family and servants alike, so that everything would be executed as efficiently and as elegantly as possible.

The Governor of Salé, Jarmun, heard about Al-Jawra'i's choice of Ibn al-Hafid's house for his guest visit; all of which made him even more resentful of the Judge, since he was bound to make full use of the honor to challenge his authority and lessen his prestige. The Governor was hell-bent on gaining complete control of this city of Salé to which he had been appointed a year earlier as a reward for betraying his own tribe. He had played a trick on them and thus inflicted a major defeat in a battle that had finally relieved the Sultan of the problems they had been causing him for some twenty years. But in spite of everything, Jarmun lost no time in assembling a welcoming party consisting of dancers, singers, horsemen, women waving flags, professional chanters* whose trills could strike terror into people's hearts, Quran specialists and pupils from religious schools.

Thus it was that Judge Ibn al-Hafid and Jarmun the Governor rode out together to greet their distinguished guest by the banks of the River Rikrak. Both men issued instructions to the boatmen who would be in charge of ferrying the party across the river. They stood there watching as dozens of boatmen linked their tiny vessels together to form a chain at the crossing-point. The boats all had wooden dolls in them, dressed in the finest silks and wearing crowns of narcissus and anemone blossoms picked from the gardens of Salé in such a limpid spring. The two men were joined by a huge crowd of officials, there to welcome the distinguished guest: senior Judges, Muftis*, religious scholars, littérateurs, merchants, men of wealth, people renowned for their virtue and good deeds, market inspectors, trade representatives, captains of ships, veterans of campaigns in Spain or on the sea, and Governor's aides—quarter-heads and shaykhs. Everyone was stationed in his appointed place.

At sunset Judge Al-Jawra'i's procession reached the bank

Chanter: a woman who produces the sound known in Arabic as "zagharid" and often translated into English as "ululations."

Mufti: a person empowered to issue a fatwa (legal opinion.)

of the River Rikrak. He crossed in a splendid vessel pulled by six sturdy rowers. Also in the boat were Ibn al-Hafid and Jarmun, two of the distinguished guest's scribes, a high-ranking general from the Sultan's military staff who was accompanying him on this particular project, and a woman who was in charge of the Judge's household, a Sudanese woman who never left his company whether at home or away; her name was Zaydah. Once across the river, the procession reformed and made its way to the city amid a huge crowd of well-wishers. By evening prayer all Al-Jawra'i's entourage had crossed the river, twenty horsemen with their horses, and twenty servants leading mules that were loaded down with baggage, weapons, and fodder.

The senior notables entered the main reception-room in Ibn al-Hafid's riyad, where the sunset prayer was said. They held back on serving drinks, sweetmeats, dried fruit, and a variety of other delicacies till the Judge arrived; in fact, he kept them all waiting for over an hour. He had gone to the public baths to rid himself of the dirt and aggravation of the journey. Once there he found that he was able to relax under the capable hands of an expert masseur from Salé, so much so, in fact, that he had it in mind to ask Ibn al-Hafid to let him take the man back to Fez on a permanent basis; now more than ever his body seemed to crave the relaxation that a good massage could provide. Meanwhile Zaydah stood by the entryway to the men's baths inside the riyad waiting for her master to emerge; with her she had brought the appropriate garments, along with the required quantities of ointments, creams and lotions.

At first the conversation focused on Al-Jawra'i's recent successes in the mission which had led the Sultan to dispatch him to Tamisna, namely to reach a peace agreement between two tribes that had taken up arms against each other in a dispute over how they were to share the burden of the new taxes that the Sultan had imposed. Afterwards the talk turned to banter involving exotic tales and citations of poetry. The company tried to outdo each other in citing literary bonmots, witty anecdotes, and all manner of abstruse quotations, all in order to show off the breadth of their learning. At one point the Judge himself took the initiative in lowering the tone of the proceedings by citing two risqué verses by Ibn al-Hajjaj; with that cue Ibn al-Hafid signaled to a young student from Salé who was a specialist in this particular repertoire to provide the assembly with some more examples of poetry that would keep things informal while not in any way detracting from the dignity of the Sultan's Chief Judge nor removing his discretion in leading the conversation.

The distinguished guest now gave permission for dinner to be brought in. Two female servants brought in the washing basin: one of them, a young girl from Sudan, was carrying the bowl itself, while the other, a gorgeous blonde, was holding the ewer and had some white towels on her shoulder. Actually, Ibn al-Hafid was not expecting this blonde servant-girl, whose name was Shamah, to make an appearance at this particular assembly. However, he could hardly send her out, since she was already in the middle of the room and had immediately attracted the attention of every man there. It was while serving in his household that she had now blossomed into womanhood. Her father was a poor widower who served as chief cowherd at his farm on the outskirts of Salé. Malicious gossip had warned the Judge that this man was actually the grandson of a Christian from West Spain; his tall stature, slim physique, clear skin, blond hair, and blue eyes all confirmed it. Shamah's mother had died when she was young, but even before then she had been brought up in Ibn al-Hafid's house. Had she come from some more illustrious ancestry, she could have been a worthy companion of amirs*.

Even so, when it came to household management, intelligence, polite conversation, and amiability, all combined with a reasonable acquaintance with matters legal and literary,

---

Amir: an Arabic word, implying commander of an army or prince/ruler of a region governed by a dynasty or family.

Shamah proved to be the accomplished pupil of the Judge's senior wife, Al-Tahirah, who lavished all her affection on her and never deprived her of anything that her own daughters had, apart, that is, from the fact that the daughters did not have to do any work and were totally cosseted. All that only served to spoil the daughters, while the need to work caused Shamah's star to wax till in the prime of her youth she became the focal point of the jealousy of every woman in the household, save for its mistress, Al-Tahirah. At the same time she was the focus of male lust, not least of Dahman, the Judge's eldest son, who kept trying to devise a way of persuading his father one day to let him take Shamah as a second wife.

Ibn al-Hafid conjured up all kinds of conspiracy-theory in order to explain how Shamah had come to make an appearance in this particular assembly without any instructions from him. But all he could do was to control his temper and keep a careful eye on things.

As the guest of honor, Al-Jawra'i was the first to have the washing bowl placed in front of him. He stretched his hands out to the water and raised his eyes to the heavens. All of a sudden he leapt to his feet with a yell. "Good heavens!" he exclaimed, "the cursed girl has scalded me!"

Ibn al-Hafid immediately went over to see what the

problem was. He found Al-Jawra'i on his feet, taking the bowl away from Shamah. Torn by the conflicting demands of pain, infatuation and politesse, he was asking Shamah to sit in his place while he poured water on her hands. What had actually happened was that, without Shamah even being aware of it, the water in the bowl had been overheated. Even so, the gleam on Al-Jawra'i's face and the way he was laughing and acting so playfully made it clear to Ibn al-Hafid that the incident would only enhance the jollity of the evening. The Judge's jocular demeanor was also enough to calm Shamah down; needless to say, the entire thing had caused her infinite embarrassment, and she had turned beet red.

Her master, Ibn al-Hafid, told her to do as the Judge ordered and sit in his place so that he could pour the water on her hands. That's exactly what he did, and Shamah recovered at least some of her poise; the water was still hot enough to hurt, but it was not scalding.

The two servant-girls withdrew and two male servants brought in another basin. The entire assembly burst into laughter. The incident was subject to a lot of comment, and lines of poetry were cited. Dinner tables were set up, and afterwards bowls with all kinds of fruit juice and syrup. Judge Al-Jawra'i did not allow the conversation to veer away from what Shamah had done to him; indeed such was his jocularity that he demanded compensation. The legal experts present competed with each other to identify the most appropriate request. Just then, Al-Jawra'i clapped his hands, whereupon the entire company fell silent to listen attentively to what the Judge had decided. "I want you all to witness," said the Judge, "that I hereby present my dear friend, Ibn al-Hafid, with a request for the hand of my foe, Shamah, in marriage. I've brought with me some dinars from the new minting of Our Lord, the Sultan, so I can pay the dowry in advance. All her guardian has to do is to agree that the wedding should take place tonight."

Ibn al-Hafid was the first to realize that the Sultan's Judge meant everything he said. His hand-clapping signaled the end of all jesting and tomfoolery. The way he had addressed him as "my friend" was obviously a trick dreamed up by one of the Sultan's advisers who held a grudge against him. Any attempt to decline the request or make fun of it might well lead to disaster. So all he could say by way of reply was: "My Lord, we'll send our fastest rider to bring her father from his house on the city outskirts; it will take an hour."

Ibn al-Hafid only just managed to avoid bursting into tears as he went into the house to inform his senior wife of what had just happened. It did not take them long to discover that his junior wife, his son's bride, and some of the servants had concocted the entire conspiracy against Shamah.

Shamah meanwhile entered her mistress's quarters and sat on the edge of her bed. Al-Tahirah did not give her the chance to burst into tears, but merely told her to get herself dressed and to muster all the sang-froid that the occasion clearly demanded. She then told two of her servant-girls to accompany Shamah to the baths because she was going to marry the Judge that very night. She then ordered two other servant-girls to make a selection from her daughters' dresses, jewelry, make-up, and perfumes of the items that would be most appropriate for the ceremony.

Shamah's father, whose name was Al-`Ajjal, arrived without knowing why he had been summoned in this fashion. He too was taken to the baths to be scrubbed clean and rid of the smell of animal dung. They dressed him in a garment supplied by the Judge, then took him to see Shamah's mistress, Al-Tahirah, whom he held in the greatest respect because of her love for his daughter. She it was who informed him that his daughter, Shamah, was to be married to the Sultan's Judge. He was then taken to see his daughter who was having her hair dressed. Hugging her to himself, he burst into tears.

Once the guardian's permission had been given and

the amount of the dowry determined, the wedding ceremony was conducted. Al-`Ajjal left with a purse full of gold, but he was still heart-broken. His chief fear was that he would never see his beloved daughter again. The guests all congratulated the Judge and then said their farewells. Judge Ibn al-Hafid took his leave too, but only after the Sultan's counselor had informed him about the nuptial feast that would be celebrated next day either by the Great Waterpool or else outside the city in the Gardens. The Judge's departure was set for the third day.

Judge Al-Jawra'i's Ṣudanese servant, Zaydah, now entered to kiss her master's foot and offer him her congratulations. She took him to the room where his bride was awaiting him on a bed with gilded posts and silken covers. Zaydah then left the room and silenced the group of women who were celebrating the marriage by banging tambourines outside the bridal suite. She was unusually brusque with them, and they scurried away without reward, their curiosity thwarted. Zaydah was so exasperated that she dragged a bed over to the doorway and went to sleep on it. A short while later the entire mansion was totally quiet and dark; no one acquainted with normal custom would have even realized that a wedding had taken place.

Al-Jawra'i now took out from his pocket a small stone

that he used for performing his ritual ablutions. He rubbed it and then prayed two rak`ahs*. All the while, Shamah, her face covered with a silk veil, watched him through a gap in the curtains. Al-Jawra'i now got into bed and took off the veil so he could look at her face. She was about to kiss his hand, but he withdrew it. He started putting her at ease, asking her about the hot water, about her mistress and the other women in Ibn al-Hafid's household, about her dead mother, her father's origins, Dahman's marriage to the daughter of a Bani Hilal shaykh from one of the Western tribes. He wanted to know every detail about her life; he was astonished to learn that she could play the lute, that she could read, and had memorized both Andalusian poetry and surahs* from the Quran.

Shamah now began to feel somewhat less apprehensive. To a certain extent the total panic that had gripped her during the abrupt preparations for the marriage and overwhelmed her capacity for clear thinking now dissipated. Like some inspiration from the beyond, she came to realize that, in exchange for one master, Ibn al-Hafid, who had given her so much attention since she was a child, she had now acquired

---

Rak`ah: literally, the process of prostration during Islamic prayer, but also used to describe a unit of prayer, involving standing, kneeling, full prostration, and then resumption of the standing position.

Surah: a segment (chapter) of the Quran.

another who would give her just as much care and affection. She suddenly noticed that he was staring at his wife as he was supposed to: taking her by the hand he asked her to stand up. He saw what he wanted to see, then bent over as though in prayer. He mumbled a few words, then burst into tears. He started mouthing complaints to his Lord God, sobbing and agonizing as he did so, as though he wished to sever limb from limb. Then in the same muted tones he begged his Lord's forgiveness, but soon reverted to his previous state of agitation, staring off into the beyond as though at some distant mountain, then lowering his gaze in shame. Shamah watched all this in total amazement, not knowing what to do; when he lowered his gaze, she would stare at him, and whenever he looked at her, she in turn would look down. She completely failed to comprehend what she was seeing and hearing. With the approach of dawn the intensity of his emotion got the better of him; he bowed his head, lowered his voice, and surrendered to a deep sleep.

Next day Shamah kept recalling fragmented images from the events of her wedding night. Even though she had no expertise in such matters, she surmised that the great Judge's rock-firm personality had dissolved in a cup a water that she herself held in her right hand and that the days ahead would be shrouded in obscurity.

Next day too, Zaydah, senior servant of Judge Al-Jawra'i, took control of things, supervising the timing and making all necessary arrangements for the wedding celebration which was to take place by the Great Waterpool in the city. Ibn al-Hafid placed himself at her disposal; after hearing her requirements, he issued orders to his family and servants. Governor Jarmun was informed of those arrangements that particularly concerned him. Zaydah would allow only two servants to assist her in bringing the bridal pair to the baths and in supervising hair-dressing, make-up and perfume, and jewelry—making sure that the bride looked her very best.

As the procession made its way through the city, it was greeted by large crowds; it kept detouring so as to pass by various shrines on its way to the Great Waterpool. Tents had been erected in one corner of the space, by the pool, well, and fountain; men were in one part and women in another. A special pavilion was designated for the bride and her coterie. Two young girls took Shamah's hand and sat her on a lofty seat which looked like the preacher's pulpit in a mosque. There she sat surrounded by her maids of honor, all decked out in their finery to replicate the practice in the most noble of households. She was wearing a heavy gown which her mistress, Al-Tahirah, had given her; her own daughters had also worn it for their own marriages. What made the dress so heavy was that it was embroidered with a gold thread known as "Sicilian"; and what made it still heavier were criss-crossed shoulder-straps of blue, purple, and pink silk. The gold necklaces she wore were encrusted with various precious stones. So slim was her waist that the gold belts caused her no problem even though they were very wide. Her drop-earrings reached to mid-neck; with all their delicate tracery and tiny encrusted jewels, both pointed and pyramid-shaped, they glistened in the light. Her bracelets were also heavily decorated, hollow on the inside in accordance with the latest fashion developed by Jewish craftsmen for the Sultan's harem and imitated by jewelers for certain members of the nobility. Thin anklets made of decorated gold-plate adorned her ankles to the point where her pantaloons reached. She wore a solitary gold ring on the middle finger of her right hand and two silver ones on the ring-finger of her left. She was also wearing an embossed hat, the base of which was enveloped by a crown of delicate gold thread and fine emeralds. At the central point of this hat Shamah's hair had been carefully gathered together by the hairdresser in a way that amply demonstrated how accomplished she was at her craft; the purpose was to emphasize both the length of the drop-earrings and Shamah's long, ivory-white neck whose exquisite beauty was only enhanced by the dark hair-roots that sprouted at the back of her neck.

Just one day earlier this entire collection of jewelry, one that was regarded with awe and reverence by the servant-women charged with its care, had been kept safely in its proper boxes and cases. Only two women who were close confidantes of their mistress, Al-Tahirah, were allowed to touch, dust, or polish the items: they were Al-Khawdah and Shamah. And now here was Shamah decked out in all this finery. Never in her wildest dreams had she ever imagined that she would be married so quickly or that her husband would be a close confidant of the Sultan himself, with the result that she was now wearing all this gorgeous jewelry, all these guests had gathered, and a group of her former mistress's servant-girls were now acting as bridesmaids with her as the bride.

Shamah scrupulously avoided thinking about such things and refused to let herself feel either pleased or shocked by what had happened. As she sat there surveying the scene through a black silk veil that further enhanced her beautiful face, her noble brow still topped by the gorgeous crown, she fastened her gaze on something that was happening at a point where the edge of the carpet met the roots of a date-palm that was shading her seat. A colony of ants was making its way to and fro from its hole (which seemed to be under the palm-tree) to its target collection point somewhere in the midst of this huge area which by now had been converted before her very eyes into a space for performance troupes. Shamah kept watching the ants as they made their way through the glistening moss. There they all were, working incessantly, just as she had done all her life, with no pause for rest. Her only goal had been to satisfy her masters. All these ants were hard at work. Inside the hole there were probably no ants either asleep or issuing orders while everyone else broke their backs working; no, they were all doing the same work and at the same speed. Who, I wonder, tells ants to start or stop working; who plans the route, works out the limits, and divides up the victuals? One indicator of difference among ants is that their stomachs are not the same size. How wonderful it would be if humans could listen to ants talking. No doubt, conversation would be restricted to the most important matters; idle chatter would be avoided at all costs. Best of all would be to listen to market-talk among ants. They clearly love life and fear death, because that is in the Quran. In fact Shamah had heard the tale of Solomon and the ants many times from the preacher who would regularly sit behind a curtain and talk to Ibn al-Hafid's womenfolk. Shamah thought about this link between love of life and fear of death, indeed between love and fear in general. It was only when she realized that she herself could not answer a crucial question as to whether she could love anyone or was afraid of anything that she finally returned to reality and suddenly became aware of her surroundings again. She heard Al-Jawra'i's voice raised in the distance, easily distinguishable from that of other people. One moment he was laughing loudly, but then suddenly he stopped. He had heard the mournful cooing of a dove sitting on the branch of a willow-tree over the pavilion that had been put up for him. He signaled to everyone to be silent; even the singers were told to stop. As everyone listened to the bird, Al-Jawra'i recited this poem:

Many's the dove that ere noon
Chants its mournful song on a branch.
Perhaps my tears disturbed its sleep,
Perhaps its tears did mine.
Should she sing first, I accompany her;
If I start, then she accompanies me.
She may cry, but I understand her not;
Should I cry, she understands me not.
Through mournful strains however I know
of her
And she likewise also knows of me.

Al-Jawra'i then gestured to Judge Ibn al-Hafid. "Learned scholar," he asked, "where is our father-in-law, Shamah's father? I would like his permission to change Shamah's named to Warqa' [dove]." After a short pause, he went on: "So he has given his permission, God preserve him! Take some newly minted dinars and use them to purchase a fat sheep so that we can proclaim my wife's new name. Sacrifice the sheep, and then give the rest of the dinars to the beggars in the city shrines. I believe one of them had a dream last night in which he imagined that from the vast regions of the unknown he was going to eat some strips of lamb." With that Al-Jawra'i stood up, kissed his wife, Shamah's, brow, and then made his way back to his seat. "And now, you singers and musicians," he said, laughing heartily as he walked, "continue with your merry-making!"

There now followed different types of singing and performance; there was more excellent food too. Later everyone prepared to return to Judge Ibn al-Hafid's riyad. In anticipation Zaydah had ordered the entire household of Ibn al-Hafid and the wives of all the notables in attendance to go on ahead and make ready to greet Judge Al-Jawra'i's new wife and kiss her hand. Under the eagle-eye of Zaydah and the Judge himself, all these ladies were forced to do so; for many of Shamah's former mistresses, the very thought was one that stuck in their craw. However, when it was the turn of Al-Tahirah, senior wife of Judge Ibn al-Hafid, it was Shamah who, with eyes welling up with tears, stood up and embraced her in a manner far beyond what the niceties of the occasion warranted.

CHAPTER TWO

Next day at dawn, Judge Al-Jawra'i's retinue left Salé; his wife, Warqa' was riding in a hawdah*. They spent the night in Tafilalet, sleeping in goat-hair tents, something that had a profound effect on Warqa' since it took her back to her childhood days on the outskirts of Salé. Al-Jawra'i spent the night checking on the tribes whose leaders had been summoned to meet him on his return journey to Fez. Warqa' did not sleep much either, because Zaydah took it upon herself to tell her everything about the Judge, and his wives and children. She told Warqa' that in Fez she would have her own quarters, but that she, Zaydah, would not be in charge. She explained that her status within the Judge's household made such a plan impossible: she had the exclusive task of accompanying him whenever he traveled and supervising all aspects of hospitality connected with the affairs of the capital city.

Once Zaydah had finished her account and fallen asleep,

Hawdah: an enclosed framework on a camel for women riders.

she spent the rest of the night snoring loudly. Warqa' found herself enveloped by an unsettling silence, only broken by the steady noise of Zaydah's snores, the padding of guards' feet as they paced to and fro among the tents, and the occasional bleat or moo from animals not far away.

Next day the retinue traveled from Tafilalet to Makhadah in the Wadi Baht near Aguray, the Judge's home territory where his family still lived. At dawn the company moved towards Aguray. A messenger had been sent on ahead to announce the imminent arrival of the tribe's protector and object of pride, Judge abu Salim Al-Jawra'i himself. Marquees had been erected, and the tribe's notables were all prepared to welcome back the Sultan's counselor whom his people commonly referred to as the "minister". From Zaydah Warqa' had learned as much as there was to know about the Judge's life: how he had left the region as a youth, studied in Fez, then Sabtah*, then Granada; how he had spent two years in Egypt and then returned to the Maghrib where he had joined the Sultan's service as supervisor of all lands held under religious endowments. After that he had worked in the judiciary in the capital city, where as a result of his astute judgment the Sultan had made him a personal counselor. He had managed to successfully complete a number of tasks that

---

Sabtah: (Ceuta) a city on the Northern coast of Morocco, still under Spanish control.

the Sultan had assigned to him in the various regions of the Maghrib and in Andalus; he had played an especially notable role in the defense of the Andalusian fortresses.

Having now arrived among the people of Aguray Warqa' was astonished to find the Judge removing her veil; it was almost as though it might somehow detract from the esteem she would gain from his aunts on both sides of the family, they being totally unfamiliar with the veil. He took her hand and presented her to his uncles who were tribal shaykhs and to his female relatives. That was how she discovered that these folk had no use whatsoever for the kind of veiling that she had encountered not merely among the notables of Salé itself but also in the cities that she had visited as part of Judge Ibn al-Hafid's retinue.

Warqa' was even more surprised when the Judge stood up and joined in all the songs and dances that the people of Aguray put on in a big square space amid the goat-hair tents with their multicolored posts. Not only that, but he dragged Warqa' herself into the circle; she kept stumbling over the skirts of her full-length silk dress from the city, while the Aguray women could dance in their shorter burnuses* which only reached mid-calf.

Burnus: a hoaded cloak or outer garment.

Warqa' noticed how very handsome these people were, men and women alike. Straight-backed and smooth-skinned, they were pure-blooded, so that red and white coloring blended to give them wonderfully ruddy complexions on both face and wrists.

Their hair was thick; with women it reached down to their waists or lower; men had curls down to their necks. Now she was almost certain she could understand why the Judge had been so taken by her at the very first glance. For someone like him, brought up in such an environment, she represented the woman of his dreams. If instead he had brought home one of the pallid, wilting demoiselles from the shady women's quarters of city riyads, he would certainly have never dared to parade her before his own folk like this. Till she was seven years old, she and her family had moved around the pastures in the forest close to Salé. She clearly belonged to precisely the same kind of folk as were embracing her now. She had every right to throw all the abuse she had received right back in the faces of the petty-minded women of Ibn al-Hafid's mansion who had insulted her by saying she was actually the child of a Christian sailor from West Spain and her grand-father had served him in Salé until his death. These jealous hussies knew absolutely nothing about what went on beyond the walls of the city. Indeed some of them had been born in Ibn al-Hafid's riyad and would die and be buried there; they would not even have a grave in the public cemetery between the city walls and the sea.

Late in the afternoon the company left Aguray for Fez and arrived at the capital city just as dawn was breaking. On the city outskirts Warqa', Zaydah and some escort guards split off from the rest of the group and headed for the East Gate. As they made their way through narrow alleys still lit by hanging lanterns, the passages were so narrow that the group had to move in single file. They stopped by a door where a muscular black servant was pacing back and forth as though waiting for their arrival. One of the two escorts spoke to him, and Warqa' heard Zaydah call him by name, Fatih; that made her feel more comfortable. He now banged on the door, and it was opened from the inside. Instructing the two escorts to bring in all the boxes from the mules' backs, Zaydah went in and was followed by Warqa'. Inside two servant-girls were waiting; one of them started trilling for joy, but Zaydah told her to stop.

By now it was daylight. The house was actually smaller than the smallest section of Ibn al-Hafid's mansion, but it was just as beautifully decorated: different types of mosaic, delicate columns, splendid doors for the four salons that opened out on to a central courtyard in which there were three pools filled with flowers, each one with an ancient figtree in the middle. Rabi`ah, the younger of the two servants, now came forward and escorted her mistress, Warqa', to the central room that had been made ready to serve as her principal abode and bedroom (since this particular house was not suitable for receiving guests). In the far corner of the room was a gold-canopied bed no less resplendent that the one Al-Tahirah, her former mistress and senior wife of Ibn al-Hafid, had in her quarters. So here she was, now able to behave as the mistress of her own household whereas previously she had had to clean and rearrange things every day for people who had found it amusing to make fun of her. Warqa', or Shamah as she then was, had previously displayed a certain reverence and respect in her dealings with such matters, all coupled with a sense of decorum and love for her mistress, Al-Tahirah. Yet she still relished that special aura that Ibn al-Hafid managed to impart to every single member of his household.

At this point however sheer exhaustion overwhelmed all other emotions. She took off everything except undergarments light enough to sleep in and left everything else to arouse the curiosity of all those around her. Once she had made sure that the servant-girl had left and closed the door behind her, she fell asleep on the carpet alongside the bed.

It was already noon when she woke up, her mind still

full of a whole cluster of images involving everything that had occurred since the night when Al-Jawra'i had visited Ibn al-Hafid's house in Salé. She stared at the ceiling with its wooden tracery, as though trying to defer any previous judgments on the course of her life. Throwing off the covers, she got into the bed to give the impression she had slept in it. Without thinking she clapped her hands, just like her former mistress in Salé, to summon the maid at such times; she was well aware that such moves and gestures were a common language in houses and on occasions such as this one. Indeed here came Rabi`ah easing her way into the room and closing the aperture in the big door so that the daylight would not dazzle her mistress's eyes which might not yet be adjusted to the glare.

Such was Warqa's innate intelligence and previous experience with household procedures that she realized that on this particular day it was crucially important that she play to the full the role of superior mistress with a group of servant-women whose equal she had herself been till just a few days earlier. Should she fail to do so, it would be a mistake that would be difficult to undo. She was comforted by the knowledge that she had all the prerequisites to carry out the function: a generous nature honed and refined by her long service with her previous mistress, Al-Tahirah; a bewitching beauty attested to by even the most jealous of her entourage;

and, above all, the total infatuation of Al-Jawra'i himself.

Rabi`ah informed her that everything was ready: bath and lunch. Warqa' went into the bathroom, but would not allow Zubaydah, the second servant-girl, to wash her; indeed she told her to leave. Once she had bathed, chosen her dress, put on some jewelry and a bit of make-up and perfume, she sat at the table and ate her lunch with relish.

As she performed her prayers, she recalled her mistress Al-Tahirah's extreme piety, since she, Shamah, was the one who had seen to her ritual cleansing and prayed with her every day at dawn. It was her prayers that undoubtedly contributed to the good fortune that had now come to her. As these thoughts went through her mind, she was overcome by emotion, and tears welled up in her eyes. However, the main emotion she felt was not happiness, but rather fear. Nothing about her recent fate gave her any comfort. True enough, the speed at which she had changed her status from servant-girl to wife of the Sultan's chief counsellor did not have its expected impact on her because her tutelage at the hands of Al-Tahirah had given her a degree of self-respect. She had spent her childhood and teenage years in the company of Ibn al-Hafid's daughters, and thus had already had occasion to witness this kind of abrupt marriage. Even so, Shamah had still not fully managed to take in what had happened to her.

What particularly bothered her was the way she had been so forcibly pulled out of the very soil where her emotions had been fostered. Now she had been snatched away, perhaps forever, from people who cared deeply about her and loved her very much.

In spite of all this Warqa' was quite spontaneous with her servant-women, not displaying the slightest sign of weakness. She did not ask a single question, but instead chose to wander around the house for herself, inspecting its various nooks and crannies and examining the facilities. Beyond that she did not feel the need for any other information. However she was still troubled by conflicting emotions and worries: that she would now be forced to sit back and do nothing, when previously she had been the one to convert immaculate service into her principal source of pleasure and self-satisfaction, especially out of loyalty to her mistress, Al-Tahirah. Would her days now be turned into a kind of living hell, she wondered, as she herself was served by two women who could not possibly earn her pleasure or trust until she had revealed to them all the secrets of her heart!

Late in the afternoon Warqa' was examining some embroidered napkins in the towel closet when Rabi`ah came in to see her. Even though there was no need for secrecy, the servant whispered in her ear that Fatih, who served the dual role of doorman and handyman for the house, wanted to give her a message that his master, Al-Jawra'i, had asked him to deliver. However, the crafty servant went on to give her a detail which explained the reason for the whisper: "Fatih is a eunuch," she said, " so he can enter your quarters." That remark earned her a disgusted look from Warqa', one that made her lower her gaze and leave.

Fatih, the man she had spotted by the entrance that morning, came in and greeted her respectfully. Once he was sure the two servants had left, he told her that his master was in attendance on the Sultan; once he had been granted permission to enter the royal presence and had been allowed to leave, he would come to see her. Such news was nothing new for Warqa' who during her time in Salé had learned that being in the Sultan's service was rather like having a second wife, something that could easily disrupt the life of spouses in their beds. Husbands would be expected to go away on missions and deputations, wait for long hours at the thresholds of throne-rooms, and take part in deliberations and wars. However two things served to mitigate her secret unhappiness and allow her to display a degree of insouciance: first, the servant-girl had told her this man was a eunuch; and second, Fatih had clearly stated that his master would be coming to see her. Even if he did come, it would only be for a short visit.

On Warqa's third afternoon in Fez, some packages were delivered containing varieties of food and provisions. A locked box was carried to Warqa's room, although she was not given the keys or told what was in it.

At sunset on the same day Warqa' heard a noise inside the house, then heard the two servants greeting someone in a manner to which she was not accustomed. Looking out through the aperture she saw her husband, Al-Jawra'i, coming across the courtyard towards her room. He signaled to her to go back inside, then entered and greeted her warmly. She was on the point of kissing his hand, but he stopped her and sat down. First by way of apology he explained why he had been unable to come before. He then stood up and prayed the sunset prayer. When he clapped his hands, the two servants entered; he gave them permission to bring in food and drink. For the first time Warqa' watched as her husband ate and drank with relish. She put on a show of eating with him as he had requested, but in fact she was so overcome with emotion and so busy watching him that she did not feel like eating anything; it was as though she were meeting him for the very first time. Several times he handed her some morsels of food which she took and ate, or else put in a bowl without him noticing. Once he had finished eating he allowed them to bring in a basin, all of which reminded her of the incident with the hot water in Salé. She stifled a laugh at the thought.

He then got up and stretched out on the bed while she sat silently on the carpet alongside.

Al-Jawra'i picked up a book from the dresser and started reading (or pretending to do so). Several times Warqa' watched him raise his eyes from the book in order to take a look at her. After a while he got up and went over to the box that had been brought in earlier in the afternoon. He opened it. It was full of all kinds of gifts, clothes, jewelry, and things that brides want to have. No sooner had the muezzin* announced the call to evening prayer than Al-Jawra'i went over to the other side of the room and performed the ritual prayer at a certain pace. Once finished, he went back to Warqa' and asked her to stand up, just as he had on their wedding night. He gazed at her body as he was entitled to do, and then once again commenced a string of impassioned verbiage, full of pleadings and apologies for something inexpressible. Bursting into tears again he demanded things that Warqa' fulfilled without hesitation. She now realized that she had to treat him like a young child who expects everything from its mother while she gets nothing in return. Relying on her common sense and her increasing feelings of affection towards him, she decided to try calming him down; his heartbeat was so fast that she was afraid for him. Just then

---

Muezzin: the person charged with reciting the call to prayer in a mosque.

his strength gave out, and he fell into a deep slumber.

For an entire month after Warqa's arrival in Fez, her husband Al-Jawra'i visited Warqa's house twice a week or more. Every time he behaved the same way; his crazy reactions only intensified, while for her part Warqa' used all of her tender affection to soothe his frenzied mixture of passion and despair. By now she had become quite used to performing this function although she still had no idea what made it necessary. Her own private hell resided in the sense of complete alienation that enveloped her. There was no one to consult about the problem, no one to serve as an appropriate confidante for her secret. Her intuition and innate decency both left her in no doubt that Al-Jawra'i loved her more than seemed possible and that through her this person who possessed everything was desperately seeking something he himself did not have. That was sufficient for her to regard him as the source of her own pleasure; in spite of everything he was lavishing on her and putting into words, he was still living a private tragedy of his own since in the end he was unable to provide her with the ultimate pleasure.

Then came the day when Warqa' ate her lunch and then got up to take a nap, something which had become a new habit of hers. Hardly had she lain down before she started to feel a pain in her stomach. When the pain got worse, she got up to boil some thyme that she could drink in a solution. The two servant-women had gone out to the quarter baths together, so she was alone in the house. However Warqa's bowels started giving out, and she lost all self-control. She started crying and groaning. When the pain got worse, she began to shout and shriek; it was so intense that she was writhing and twisting. When Fatih came in and found her in this state, he went running out. One hour later he came back with the Judge and a Jewish doctor from the Fez hospital called Ibn al-Zarah.

The two servant-women had returned before the Judge and doctor arrived and discovered that Warqa' had fainted from the sheer pain. They had laid her out on the bed. The doctor informed the Judge that she had been poisoned and was close to death; the foam on her lips made that much clear. He sent out for some drugs; meanwhile he poured a liquid into her mouth to bring her round; all that took a whole hour of bleeding and massage, but eventually he succeeded. Once again she started twisting in agony. Now he poured some soap-solution into her mouth. No sooner had it settled in her stomach than she sat bolt upright and spewed a powerful torrent of vomit all over the doctor and those around him.

All the while the Judge kept looking at Warqa's face and encouraging the doctor. He asked a whole host of questions, then sat on the carpet weeping with his head in his hands. He forgot all about self-respect; with the Jewish doctor there such things did not matter, and he had nothing to be jealous about. Where the servant-women were concerned, their lives were in his hands if they were the slightest bit indiscreet.

It was late at night by the time the doctor finally managed to extract all the poison from Warqa's stomach. The Judge was assured that she would live, although there might be other consequences—loss of hair, pallor, and emaciation for a certain period. Warqa', still semi-comatose, was given some liquid nourishment to build up her strength. With that they left her to sleep.

The Judge was fully aware which particular sector in his life it was that needed investigating in order to determine what had happened. He charged Fatih and one of his most trusted retainers with the task. Al-Jawra'i returned next day at noon to find that Warqa' had woken up but was too weak even to move her hands. Fatih and the other retainer informed him that, faced with the direst threats, the two servant-women had confessed to their crime. They had replaced the tray of meat sent from the neighborhood oven with another one. The poisoning had been arranged by Al-Jawra'i's wife, the mother of his children; she had been hatching the plot ever since she had learned of Warqa's arrival in Fez.

The Judge sat in the middle of the house. He gave orders for the two servant-women to be taken and sold to the traders who transport slaves of all kinds from the Maghreb to the Sudan. He then asked for pen, paper, and inkwell and wrote as follows:

To our beloved friend, Abu al-`Abbas Ibn al-Hafid, Judge of Salé: Greetings to you! With the arrival of this letter, send us as soon as possible a skilled servant-woman to whom can be entrusted the care of Warqa'. Farewell!

CHAPTER THREE

A week later Al-Jawra'i's emissary returned to Fez with Al-Khawdah, one of the servant-women of Al-Tahirah, mistress of Ibn al-Hafid's household. Al-Khawdah found Warqa' still confined to her bed; fully a third of her hair had fallen out. Al-Khawdah burst into tears, but Warqa' was delighted to have a companion, something she had never even dreamed of; she was fully aware that this gesture, sending her most beloved servant-woman to be with her in Fez, was yet another act of kindness on the part of her mistress, Al-Tahirah.

It took a whole day and night for Warqa' and Al-Khawdah to exchange news about what had been going on in both Salé and Fez after Warqa's departure. In Ibn al-Hafid's household the most important event had been that the Judge had taken his revenge on the ladies and servants who had planned the entire incident with the boiling water. Once it became clear that it was the wife of his son, Dahman, who had been the major mover in the plot, she had been divorced from him and sent back to her family. The Judge had asked Shamah's father to give up his job herding cattle on the city outskirts and instead either to devote himself to a life of prayer in the mendicants' shrine with a guaranteed income from the Judge himself or else to sit himself on a bench in his house and serve as a counselor. However her father refused the Judge's offers and insisted on staying where he was. Meanwhile, as day followed day, Jarmun, the Governor of Salé, continued to devise numerous ways of oppressing the people of the city. For her part, Al-Khawdah teased Warqa' by telling her how the women who were jealous of her good fortune had changed her name from Warqa' to Warka' [cripple]. However what gave her the most gratification was that her mistress, Al-Tahirah, had been thrilled. In front of everyone she had stated that Shamah's good fortune had come about as a result of her own prayers; it was all a reward for Shamah's loyalty and her unique qualities which were a gift from God Himself.

Warqa' told Al-Khawdah about the journey from Salé to Fez: how much she admired Zaydah and how she had come to appreciate the men and women of Aguray during the short time the Judge's retinue had spent there. However Al-Khawdah did not let Warqa' spend too much time on such detail; her patience was wearing thin. What she really wanted to hear about was Warqa's private life with the Judge. With that, Warqa' became more agitated, threw herself into Al-Khawdah's arms, and started weeping. Al-Khawdah hugged her and tried to calm her down, assuring her that all her troubles would be lightened if only she would tell her story in detail.

So Warqa' did just that. It was not long before Warqa' started stuttering and her throat felt dry, but that was long enough for Al-Khawdah to realize what was happening. She felt a large lump in her throat and started to develop a hatred towards this lothario Judge whose behavior towards Warqa' was no different from any man with the authority to put an innocent young girl into a golden cage in order to satisfy his own ego. However, Warqa' composed herself and decided to resist this well-meaning attempt at sympathy on the part of someone who ever since her adolescence in Salé had been her close friend. She told Al-Khawdah how kind the Judge was to her, how sincere was his love, and how his childlike moods had earned her affection. She even said that she was never happier that when he managed to spend the few hours he had available by her side.

Al-Khawdah now realized that Warqa' did not want to further aggravate this wound in her heart. All she had needed was someone to share her secret with, to provide the necessary assurance when she was unsure of herself, but beyond that to keep the entire matter under wraps. In spite of differences in both age and experience, both women were sufficiently sensitive to understand the slightest gesture from the other. For her part Al-Khawdah made it her primary task to provide soothing balm for Warqa's profound sorrow.

Al-Khawdah herself had only been married to a huge ship-captain for two years, and for most of that time he had been at sea. It had been his ship-master who had bought her mother, Luhi, at the slave-market in Dir`ah when she was still pre-pubescent. He had paid a huge price for her because she was descended from the ruling Fulani family in the Sudan. When this ship-master had died, Al-Khawdah herself was ready for marriage; she was still using the Fulani language of her mother's tribe in the Sudan. Her husband had been captured by Christian sailors while she was pregnant. She had a baby girl, but her husband, named Salih, had never been ransomed and never came back. For that reason the Judge had declared her divorced. The story was that her absent husband had attacked the captain of the vessel that captured him and had killed him, whereupon the husband's captors had killed him in revenge. This story about Al-Khawdah's husband had become a heroic tale of bravery, embellished in time by all sorts of additional details to fire the imaginations of the children of Salé. At any rate, that is how Al-Khawdah and her daughter came to join Judge Ibn al-Hafid's harem.

She was nicknamed "desert gazelle," for her slim build, her delicate features, and the graceful way she moved when at work. In addition she exuded self-assurance and pride, and was scrupulous in her observance of the necessary politesses. Shamah herself would never have been able to rival Al-Khawdah's qualities if she had not first learned from her all the secret skills whereby she had mastered the requirements of household-service. To such skills Shamah added a certain spirituality fostered by the way that her mistress, Al-Tahirah, loved her. The core of that spirituality revolved around something akin to veneration for her husband, Ibn al-Hafid, and a knack for keeping his secrets and advertising his virtues.

Al-Khawdah asked Warqa' to talk about the poisoning episode. She learned how the whole thing had been planned in Al-Jawra'i's house and carried out by the two servant-women, or at least one of them. It had all happened when without the Judge's knowledge she had requested some meat cooked in the ashes of the local grill-oven.

Shamah now went into the baths and Al-Khawdah went with her because she wanted to check on her condition. She heaved a deep sigh as she looked at the fading blue blotches on her skin and the tufts of hair growing back to replace what had fallen out. Together they considered various medical emergencies they had heard about, including cases of poisoning involving an amount considerably less than the deadly powder that had been put into the meat-dish that Warqa' had eaten. They both agreed that she owed her life to the Jewish physician.

Now they both had to be on their guard against all the other conspiracies that would, no doubt, be hatched in the future. Al-Khawdah would have to know the entire domain in order to protect that person who was now her mistress. That would involve finding out about every single nook and cranny in the house, getting to know the neighbors, the city, and whichever of the Judge's retainers came to the house, and finding out precisely how the selection of food sent over to the house was made. She learned that in future Fatih the doorman would be their principal resort, so she made a point of getting to know him and engaging him in conversation so as to assess his intentions and make use of him as a source of the information she required about goings-on in the city. In Ibn al-Hafid's household she had already learned a lesson, namely that staying abreast of what was happening was the best protection against inimical intentions.

Warqa' allowed her to bang on the main door in the usual way. In came Fatih. Once he was in the central passageway between the pools he found Warqa' seated on a bench surrounded by pieces of embroidery. Once he had greeted her, she told him to help the new servant-woman in whatever way she needed. She clapped her hands to summon Al-Khawdah from the kitchen where she had concealed herself in order to get a first glimpse of Fatih. She now came out and stood in front of Fatih who lowered his eyes. She was taken aback and could not prevent a shiver from going right through her; she kept staring at him, eyes wide open, mouth agape. This supremely fit, comely man would have been a carbon-copy of her husband, were it not for the black color of his skin. Fatih went out to the front-door to tell his assistant to take over the watch, then came back to help Al-Khawdah change the water in some of the conserve jars in the kitchen. Warqa' had noticed the way Al-Khawdah had reacted to Fatih and guessed why.

"He's a eunuch," she told Al-Khawdah before she went away. "We never knew our master, Ibn al-Hafid, to own a single one, did we?"

"Rulers only castrate their assistants," retorted Al-Khawdah without giving too much thought to the impact of what she was saying, "in order to hide the fact that their own masculinity is either totally lacking or else deficient."

Even so Warqa' took Al-Khawdah's response as a sign

of the love and sympathy she felt for her. "Yes," she said, "and it's we women who bear the brunt of it!"

Al-Khawdah and Fatih spent a long time arranging the jars in the storeroom next to the kitchen. She asked a whole string of questions about any number of subjects. Eventually she told him that next day she would dress up as a normal servant-woman and get him to escort her to the major shrine in the city so that she could spend some time praying and seeking the merciful intervention of the Unseen. However Fatih told her that he could not undertake such a mission; it would require permission from his master, the Judge.

It so happened that the Judge came to visit Warqa's house that very evening. He was delighted to find his wife so full of life as a result of Al-Khawdah's arrival. He stared at the Fulani woman with the golden complexion and was aware that her movements were so graceful that you felt her feet barely touched the ground. Her sense of politesse gave credence to what Warqa' herself had already said, namely that Al-Khawdah was the accomplished mistress of every possible craft. For all these reasons the Judge himself was full of admiration and praise, along with a good deal of sympathy when he heard about the way she had lost her husband and been separated from her child who had stayed in Ibn al-Hafid's household. So as to please Warqa' the Judge promised to write to the Governor of Tarifah in Andalusia, requesting that he investigate the story about this prisoner from Salé and, if he was still alive, pay his ransom. More than that, he promised that, if it emerged that Al-Khawdah's husband was actually dead, he would see that she was properly cared for.

All that made Warqa' love her husband even more, this man whose only concern was to implement whatever might please her. At the same time she felt a twinge of jealousy, but she soon suppressed it with the thought that the Judge was no doubt planning to marry off her companion al-Khawdah to one of Fatih's own people who had not been castrated and to reunite her with her daughter in Salé.

The Judge now gave her authorization to issue whatever orders she wished Fatih to carry out. He also promised to buy her a maid from the Taza slave-market, someone who would not cause any trouble since she would have no connection whatsoever with the women who had posed such a threat to Warqa's very life.

With each passing day Warqa' put the poisoning incident behind her and recovered her radiance. Every time the Judge arrived, it was to find her in a new outfit that reflected joint planning by Warqa' and Al-Khawdah. He now felt so reassured by everything she said and did that all the twisted complexes of her tongue and heart were unraveled. From now on she could not anticipate anything offending him. Indeed there was every indication of her determination to make sure that whatever she provided for him would surpass anything he could conceive of receiving or asking for. With every visit she had something new for him, and she bestowed it all with an utter devotion and pleasure that reflected a belief in her own good fortune.

The following afternoon Al-Khawdah went out to pay her visit to the city's major shrine. As she had expected, beneath the green-tiled roof was gathered a large crowd of women who encircled the tomb, its green shroud and grilles topped by golden fronds and orbs. They were all talking to each other, but their chatter was drowned out by the noise of Quran chanters and the pleadings of sinners of every kind and the desperately sick. It was as if every one of these women supplicants had opened her bag of secrets and was sharing the contents with someone else. What was most important was that, without even being aware of it, every woman there was transformed into the spirit of the shrine's saint as she imparted to her neighbor the most effective cure for her particular problem. As a result every woman left the shrine rid of the condition with which she had entered.

Al-Khawdah approached a number of women who

seemed to be keeping their eyes wide open and to have a grip on the city's rumor-machine. These women would be the types to make their way around the city's quarters. Doors would be opened for a variety of reasons, sometimes to repair bruised emotions, at others to crush entire families. The women would purvey phony spells, serve as intermediaries with talisman-writers, and organize alternative slave-markets where the taxman and controller of public morality would not be involved. Al-Khawdah was looking for women from whom she would be able to buy information about Al-Jawra'i and his master, the Sultan himself. She did not leave the shrine until she had made sure that she had identified more than one provider of the commodity she was seeking.

When she returned to the shrine the following Friday afternoon, she took a pocketful of dirhams* with her. Beside the doorway she noticed a woman whose demeanor made it clear that she was totally unafraid of any upholders of public morality. Flaunting herself suggestively and obviously deranged, she cared nothing about those around her. In times past perhaps she had seen her glory-days as the beloved of some prince or a senior figure in this ruling family. Al-Khawdah made it her first task to find out about this brazen woman who smiled at every man going into the shrine and

---

Dirham: a unit of currency and a coin.

used her gorgeous eyes to aim killer glances at every passer-by. She was well-known, it emerged; the wife of an officer in the Sultan's guard. Her husband had taken another wife and ignored her. That had turned her into a she-devil. Every Friday she would stand by this holy entryway. People called her "guru-chaser." A particular story about her told how a devout man from the region of Jabal Azkan near Fez had been so involved in his devotions in the mountains that he could actually levitate; however, no sooner did he levitate his way down to Fez and set eyes on her than he completely lost his piety and was forced to rent a lame donkey in order to make his way back up to the mountain-top.

As a result of her excursion Al-Khawdah learned more than she anticipated about Al-Jawra'i and his household. In fact she positively shuddered when she learned from one of her informants that the Sultan himself had spent much of his latest soiree teasing Al-Jawra'i about his marriage in Fez, quoting precise details that had been forwarded to him in a letter from Jarmun, the Governor of Salé. Indeed the informant was crafty enough to close her account by saying that the Sultan had reproved Al-Jawra'i by pointing out that the Sultan's own household had no one to rival Warqa's beauty.

This informant woman was actually correct in what she reported about the way Al-Jawra'i was being teased.

The Sultan's household included a wit whose acid tongue was much feared by his senior retainers; when it came to reproach and humiliation he was a master. "Esteemed counselor," he said to Al-Jawra'i, "we gather that, when you heard the dove cooing, you recited some poetry. However, you maligned Al-Nuri by leaving out a verse which you thought would be inappropriate. Which one is it?"

Al-Jawra'i noticed that the Sultan was fully in tune with his courtier's sarcasm; there was nothing for it but to recite the verse:

> "Recalling a beloved, a time, and a devotee,
> She burst into tears, and thereby kindled my grief.

I left it out because I was afraid to predict what the future might bring."

"I wonder," the Sultan retorted, "whether she has left you any mind that can still offer me sound advice!"

The Judge was astonished by this remark. He felt as though someone had just poured freezing cold water all over him. But in spite of everything the Sultan continued to discuss important matters of government business with him in private, the kinds of thing he did not wish to share with anyone else.

Al-Khawdah returned to the house, but did not reveal to Warqa' any information that might alarm her. Even so, she resolved to herself that she would pay very close attention to every single word that Warqa' reported the Judge as uttering on his next visit.

The plan worked. What she had learned from her informant at the shrine was proved correct when Warqa' reported that the Judge seemed out of sorts on this visit. Along with all the usual ravings he kept repeating things like: "I'm afraid the wolves will get you, I'm afraid the wolves will get you..." On the next visit Warqa' told her Al-Jawra'i had started talking about the Sultan and criticizing his extravagant spending on mosque-schools; it was placing a huge strain on the treasury and would impose a heavy tax burden on the people. He also said that the Sultan was ignoring his advice by embarking on an expedition that would involve taking a large army to the Eastern provinces to bring dissident Bedouin tribes back into line. He was already getting troops and mercenaries together. He would be away from the capital city for a long time, which raised the dangerous possibility that others might be tempted to seize power, principal amongst whom was the Crown Prince who had long been eager to take his place on the throne.

At this point Al-Jawra'i broke his normal pattern by staying away from Warqa's house for two weeks. Warqa' was upset, while Al-Khawdah felt uneasy because she knew more of Al-Jawra'i's secrets that her own mistress did. Then one day at noon Al-Jawra'i paid a visit. He apologized because the need to make all the arrangements for the expedition to the Eastern provinces had kept him busy with the Sultan. He clapped his hands, and Fatih came in carrying a box full of precious trinkets. For her part, Warqa' was anxious to show her husband how happy she was with the gifts and at the same time to surprise him by demonstrating some of her skills that he had not seen before although he had already heard about them. She gestured to Al-Khawdah who brought in her guitar, it being part of her private property that had been brought from Salé. The Judge stopped drinking and followed her movements in amazement. Shamah sat on a bench, tuned the strings, and then started singing in a voice that had greatly impressed her teacher in Granada. She sang a song from her time in Ibn al-Hafid's household:

> In her image is beauty complete.
> Her waist sways while her bosom ripples.
> She stood up to walk; if only God would let me

Be that earth caressed by her feet!

The Judge got up to dance. "I am that earth," he said, "I am that earth!" He leaned over ecstatically towards Warqa' and recited:

> "From Jacob Warqa' has learned
> To weep and reveal inner secrets,
> But her singing is the art of Ishaq.*

How have you managed to keep your lovely singing a secret from me till today?!"

The Judge was so overcome that he had to look down; it was as though a wound had been reopened. Warqa's voice was just as gorgeous as she was, and he was very upset because he was incapable of showing the proper appreciation for either. Warqa' realized at once that, instead of making her husband happy, her singing had only managed to get him worked up. She switched to a sad melody and sang a song that her mistress, Al-Tahirah, used to love:

> Should fate do you ill, be steadfast,

Ishaq: a reference to Ishaq al-Mawsili (d. 849 AD), the greatest virtuoso singer in the history of Arabic culture.

For such is the believer's paradise.
Lack and plenty both come
In accordance with God's divine will.

Before departing the Judge told Warqa' that a delegation from the Sultan of Mali from the region of blacks to the south would be arriving. There would be a splendid procession bringing gifts to Our Lord the Sultan. Fatih could take them in disguise to the misriyyah* of a merchant from which they could observe the street along which the procession was to pass and enjoy the view to their hearts' content.

Warqa' was delighted by this news. She told the Judge how much she appreciated such care and attention. He was clearly well aware of the beneficial effects that Al-Khawdah's arrival in Fez had had on her own peace of mind and was trying hard to make their life together as happy as he could. The people bringing gifts to the Sultan of the Maghrib would be Al-Khawdah's own folk from her mother's family. Warqa' clapped her hands, and Al-Khawdah appeared before her. She was thrilled by this totally unexpected news. The stories her mother had told her about the land of Al-Takrur were still fresh in her mind, including the fact that she was descended from an Islamic dynasty that had for many years ruled on the

---

Misriyyah: a single-room upper story in a traditional Moroccan house.

banks of the River Niger until raiders from the desert to the North had destroyed it during a drought period, enslaved all its people—in contravention to the laws of Islam, and sold them all in the slave-markets to the North.

On the day in question, Warqa', Al-Khawdah, and the new maid were all taken to the misriyyah overlooking the parade. Disguised as Bedouin cloth-sellers, they were escorted there by Fatih. The main streets in Fez were all lined by the Sultan's guards, armed with spears and javelins. Horsemen rode up and down the streets along which the parade was to pass. The people of Fez were ranged all along the route, and the roofs of houses were filled with cloistered ladies who came from near and far. Just after noon the sound of drums could be heard, announcing the imminent arrival of the parade. The Sultan himself was anxious that this spectacle should have the required effect on his people, showing that his influence extended all the way to Mali. They would then be prepared to lend financial support to his forthcoming expedition to the eastern flank of his own territories. Success in such a venture would give a boost to further efforts aimed at securing victory in Al-Andalus.

The procession was led by the Sultan's guards wearing their full dress-uniform, playing loud tunes on their oboes. Then came the first group of blacks, semi-naked dancers, followed by drummers and brass. They were followed by carts carrying huge cages, filled with lions and other large carnivores. Then a group of slave-women, part of the gift to the Sultan, all dressed in white and wearing colored headdresses shaped like camel-humps and precious amber necklets. They were all singing a charming song and swaying to left and right while performing a fascinating dance. Their gleaming white teeth reflected the sunlight and glistened like the purest silver. Then came the giraffe, that amazing animal, so tall and lanky, striding along arrogantly and turning its head this way and that without the slightest concern for the people watching it or for anything else that might be expected to annoy or scare it. The sight of such an animal brought the excitement of the spectators to its very peak, men, women, and children alike. Behind the giraffe came a troupe of magicians wearing feather headdresses and thigh-pads of matted straw, their foreheads decorated with multicolored criss-cross designs. The gestures they were making convinced people that, if they threw down the canes they were carrying, they would change into snakes. After them came a group of fire-eaters and a troop of curassiers. The rearguard consisted of camels carrying sacks of gold intended for the Sultan.

As Warqa' and Al-Khawdah watched the procession and were stirred by the drum-beats, Warqa' altered her moods to match that of her companion, joy at times, then tears. If it had not been for the affection that the two women felt for each other, Warqa' would have been much more interested in exploring the city's alleyways than in enjoying the spectacle as the procession passed by.

Al-Jawra'i now stayed away from Warqa's house for an entire week. When he did come, it was in the very early morning; in fact, he woke her up. Once she had got up and washed herself, he asked for fruit-juice and honey. At first he joked with her about the procession from Mali, but then his expression changed. He clapped his hands to summon Al-Khawdah. "The Sultan's expedition to the Eastern sector will start in three day's time," he said. "On that day I shall be part of the advance-party that will leave Fez to prepare for the Sultan's arrival at the port from which he will be sailing. He has also requested that you, Shamah, should join his illustrious entourage for this expedition. You are therefore to travel as part of the main force; my servant-women, Zaydah, and Fatih will all be in attendance. You will share a cabin with one of the royal concubines on the ship called The King's Felicity. Al-Khawdah will return to Ibn al-Hafid's household until God grants us all a safe return."

As he conveyed this momentous news to the women, the expression on his face and the tone of voice he adopted revealed aspects of the personality of Al-Jawra'i, the Sultan's trusty counselor, that he rarely displayed. It was actually all part of his political machismo, something he could invoke whenever necessary, while suppressing all other sentiments. It was obvious that he had not come at this hour of the night simply to provide them with information about orders, every single detail of which had already been put carefully into place. As he said farewell, he managed to assure Warqa' that, even though a good deal of what he had told them was not very clear, he would protect her forever with his dying breath.

CHAPTER FOUR

The journey to the port north-east of Fez took eight days, and the sea-voyage lasted three months. The fleet kept having to put in at ports on the way and could only resume its progress when the enormous land army had covered the same distance and had made quite sure that all the tribes, governors, and allies on the route had offered appropriate levels of gifts, services, and facilities.

Warqa' now discovered the true extent of Zaydah's generosity and loyalty to her master, something she had not managed to do during their earlier journey from Salé to Fez. She also learned about the routines of life at sea: the surprises, the changing moods of winds, the harshness of captains, and the trials of rowers. She was part of a small group of extraordinarily beautiful and elegant women, all of them served by maids of equally decorous qualities whose health and grace remained unaffected by the ravages of sea-sickness.

The three ships carrying the harem, with its women of different races and colors (most of them from the royal household itself, but a few from the families of close confidants), along with the attending company of servants and eunuchs, eventually reached the largest port in the Eastern sector. Everyone disembarked and was escorted by a brigade of horsemen to a palace outside the region's capital city. Once there the women were subjected to a rigid regime: they were not allowed to mingle with women from other palaces, the only exceptions being when they went to the baths or attended spectacles that were presented in the palace's central courtyard.

Three months went by without any visits from either the Sultan or any of his senior retainers. Rumors started to spread that the Sultan's expedition had failed because he had been betrayed by some Bedouin shaykhs. The land army had made its way back to Fez, and the Sultan himself had taken his huge fleet to sea again. The harem was in imminent danger of being taken prisoner by the Sultan's enemies. The rumor spread around the palace. Then one morning the Sultan's guards gathered all the women in a circle. Two huge soldiers went over to a white woman and her black maid, dragged them into the middle of the circle, and tied their hands behind their backs. Bringing over a wooden post, they tied each woman to it and gave her twenty lashes. No explanation was given, but everyone understood that they were being held responsible for spreading the rumor that had caused so much commotion.

Following two days of dreadful panic, orders were given to leave. Warqa' boarded the first vessel to sail, an enormous, powerful boat that the Sultan was said to have hired from the ruler of Sicily. The majority of people on board were Christian captains and soldiers who spoke a mixture of languages, Arabic and others. During the course of the voyage people on board started noticing that the sea kept tossing up debris from shipwrecks: planks, expensive goods, clothing, and human corpses. This only served to upset the women even more as they worried about the fate of their husbands. After spending several days encountering all this flotsam, they began to realize that a huge storm must have come up, leading to a colossal naval disaster and the loss of a number of vessels from the Sultan's fleet. The insignia of senior army commanders were seen bobbing on the sea-surface, then a huge wooden plank which had been the name-plate of The King's Felicity; with that the weeping and wailing intensified. At this particular point, the commander in charge of the harem, a man named Ibn Mubarak, grabbed a slave-girl who was screaming loudly and held her out over the gunwales, fully intending to throw her into the sea in full view and hearing of the palace women.

The huge vessel spent several days battling rough seas. The women were not allowed up either to the upper decks or the walkway that looked out on the sea. The putrid air below decks and the turbulent swell turned the entire collection of delicate and sickly women into lifeless corpses; they could not keep anything in their stomachs. Many of them complained of headaches; some of them had a fever as well. All the suffering involved kept the servant corps fully occupied; all of which meant that, whenever the ship started tossing, pitching, yawing, stalling and twisting, they did not feel as scared as the other women. All the while none of them had any idea as to whether they were on their way home or instead had been taken prisoner by pirates, in which case they would undoubtedly be sold off at slave-markets in Christian territory or else to Bedouin gold merchants.

A group of servant-women accompanying the harem were instructed to go up to the top decks and offer the captains food and service. By listening and watching they were able to gather what it was that had led the captains to prevent the women from coming up for some fresh air. Thousands of pieces of flotsam were floating on the waves and crashing into their boat. Decorations worn by senior officers in the Muslim armies were being ripped off by the waves just as the enemy would do to the shoulder-flashes of a defeated foe. Now here was the sea behaving the same way. Pages

of Qurans and other books floated on the waves, which proceeded to devour their contents like the greatest of exegetes.
Flocks of birds hovered over the beaches or close to them,
cawing as they swooped down to peck at objects floating on
the water. The sailors who were watching knew from bitter
experience that the objects were actually human corpses.
The birds were eating parts of severed heads, a free gift presented by defeat and death's sharp fangs as tasty morsels for
the eager claws of these predators.

Truth to tell, the entire scenario had been stripped of
every vestige of merit or prestige; all that remained was fear
itself and the callousness with which the men in charge of
the harem kept trying to maintain control over the women.

When their Sicilian vessel encountered another
Christian vessel coming from the opposite direction, even
the bravest of the Sultan's guards charged with protecting the harem panicked. The two ships exchanged signals,
then the captain of the Sicilian ship got into a skiff and went
over to the other boat. The Muslims were afraid that such
communications meant that the two men would make a deal
to imprison the harem and take them to Christian territory. After fully half a day the captain returned to the vessel.
He gave Ibn Mubarak the news from Sabtah (according to
the other captain), which confirmed that the Sultan's navy

had indeed suffered a grievous loss. The only ship to reach shore had been the Sultan's own. However, his own son had meanwhile deposed him and received homage in Fez from a number of Maghribi tribes.

The commander Ibn al-Mubarak kept this piece of information to himself. Standing before one of the Sultan's wives who happened to be on board, he asked her to collect some sacks of gold in order to guarantee the continuing loyalty of the ship's captain. Agreement had been reached, he said, to convey the harem to the port of Al-Mazammah.

CHAPTER FIVE

Ten days later the harem reached Fez. Ibn al-Mubarak had been given his instructions while still in Taza. The journey was timed so that they would arrive at about midnight. Everyone now found themselves inside a palace where both procedures and faces were completely different from those they had been familiar with when they lived there.

Next day the new Sultan's officials arrived. They assembled all the women who had just returned from the Eastern sector and proceeded to implement the Sultan's orders which affected every member of the former harem. The officials involved consisted of guard-officers, jurists, and wives of the new gentry.

In a scene reminiscent of the Day of Judgment itself the women of the harem were called out, one by one, beginning with those most closely associated with the ex-Sultan. Then came the turn of the women whose husbands had been drowned in the naval disaster. At that point in time none of the women had been given any information at all. So, every time a name was called out and the woman in question realized that she was now a widow, she fainted on the spot. Then came the turn of Shamah, Al-`Ajjal's daughter and now Al-Jawra'i's widow. All she said was, "Verily to God do we belong and unto Him do we return," but otherwise she maintained her poise. She was listed as being part of the estate of her deceased husband and consigned to the new Sultan. She was instructed to don widow's garments; during the course of her waiting-period, she was to enter the service of the former Sultan's senior wife (who was not the new Sultan's mother), a lady named Umm al-Hurr.

So Shamah found herself sent to the house of the senior wife of the deposed Sultan. Once there, the housemaids warned her not to go around looking so sad; miserable expressions like hers would only spoil the jolly atmosphere which would greet the new Sultan's accession to the throne. One of them instructed her to go to the baths and change into more appropriate clothes before going that same evening to meet her new mistress, Umm al-Hurr. So, if only to suppress her grief, she went to the baths; once there, she immediately burst into tears. She told herself that the huge defeat may actually have saved her; as her late husband, Al-Jawra'i, was drowning, he was probably thinking about all the indignities she would have to suffer at the hands of the people he had called "wolves."

Her new mistress, Umm al-Hurr, bore all the trappings of royalty, a distinguished mien, penetrating gaze, and a dignity that defied age; a woman in her fifties, she was seated on a regal couch in a large room at one end of which was a bed encrusted with precious stones.

Shamah kissed her new mistress's feet. Umm al-Hurr gestured to her to sit on another couch opposite her and told everyone else to leave. From the very first moment, Shamah had no doubt in her mind that this imposing woman knew everything about her; she had selected her from among all the people in her husband's entourage who had survived the sea disaster. Umm al-Hurr showed her every kindness and made a particular effort to comfort her troubled heart by mentioning that she knew of Al-Tahirah, Judge Ibn al-Hafid's wife, who had been her protector. Nor was that all. She made it clear to Shamah that she would not be using her as a servant but rather as a confidante.

Shamah watched in admiration as this lady, the senior wife of the deposed Sultan, was the very first to eschew all bitterness and grief, thereby responding to the specific orders that had been issued to refrain from any reference, however indirect, to the era of the previous Sultan or to his disastrous expedition to the Eastern sector.

It needed just a few days for Umm al-Hurr to realize that Shamah fully deserved all the kindness and confidence that she was planning to bestow on her. Such was Shamah's beauty, refinement, and skill, not only in the way she served her mistress but also in household management—even of the entire palace—that her trust was clearly well-placed.

On more than one occasion Shamah would look up at her mistress and find her staring fixedly at her. It was as though she wanted to say something, but realized that, with the wound of Shamah's personal sorrow so fresh, the time was not yet right.

The regime in Umm al-Hurr's household involved devoting each day of the week to a particular activity. The purpose of it all was to avoid a daily routine, to seek diversion, and to perform charitable deeds appropriate to the dignity of her lofty station.

Fridays were devoted to charity. Baskets of provisions would be discreetly sent to indigents who were too ashamed to beg. Bowls of food would be dispatched to certain mosques and small amounts of cash distributed to the collection-boxes in certain shrines. Gifts would be sent to Quran readers and devout worshippers. People released from either prison or hospital would receive assistance, as would inhabitants of the lepers' quarter and the infirm. Bags of dried fruit would be distributed to children at the entrances to cemeteries.

On Saturdays Umm al-Hurr, her maidservants, and senior members of her household would all be taken to greet the Sultan. Elaborate preparations would be involved since, in accordance with the protocol of the palace, everything had to be done in the best possible taste. Umm al-Hurr's turn came after that of her former fellow-wife, the Sultan's mother, and her retinue. Following her came younger sons and daughters of the family and other close relations, all in accordance with their station. Other relatives only greeted the Sultan at festivals. As each group presented its greetings, the Sultan would ask those responsible for the budget of each household for details about income support, requirements, and absolute necessities. This would also be the occasion to present requests, and raise matters involving implementation, compensation, arbitration, and reconciliation; it was also an appropriate moment at which to mention –insofar as it did not involve a breach of etiquette—any grievances which the Sultan's judiciary had failed to resolve. The Sultan would receive condolences on the death of any close relatives. His agreement would be sought whenever a marriage or the naming of a newborn child was involved.

On Sundays Umm al-Hurr would take a promenade either in the palace gardens or else at the Sultan's estates outside the city. She would select her entourage on each occasion and suggest dishes that could be carried in pots; they would be served either in the open air or else on one of the verandas or in tents. She would often allow her maids to go down to the lake and ride around in boats pulled by squads of young men. This would be an occasion for picking the ripe seasonal fruit or gathering flowers from whose petals perfumes would be extracted.

Mondays involved assembling a number of expert women to make a wide variety of sweet-cakes and to prepare conserves for future use. Each of the women was an unrivaled expert at making a particular kind of cake; she would make every effort to embellish it either with decorations or else by devising different flavors that made use of vegetable essences and sweeteners such as cane-sugar, honey, and so on. Once the cakes had been cooked, they would be categorized according to the predominant flavor, such as sugar, salt, or tart; or else by origin: local, Muslim, Jewish, city, coast, or desert; or else by the repute of certain cities or their foreign provenance: Spanish, Eastern, Sudanese. Every woman who kept making her specialty was keen to enhance her mistress's prestige should she be asked to provide an example of her dish for some special occasion at the Sultan's household.

On Tuesdays the women of Umm al-Hurr's household indulged themselves in various kinds of entertainment. All cooking, washing and cleaning would finish at noon. Once lunch was over, drinking vessels would be put out, incense-burners would be filled, and perfume sprinklers would be prepared. They would bring in musical instruments, and young girls who had studied music and memorized tunes, segments of ancient poetry, zajal*, and tribal song would sit down. The mistress of the house would begin by indicating a song that she wanted to hear, but, more often than not, she would then allow them enough time to amuse themselves by choosing the songs they wanted. She would let them give free rein to their emotions, even to the extent of allowing them to swoon to the passionate effects of dance and infatuation. Sometimes it even happened that the Sultan's household would send a male troupe over to Umm al-Hurr's house, in which case the women would watch through upstairs windows, from balconies, or behind curtains in the evening gloom.

Zajal: a form of strophic poetry that emerged in Spain during the Muslim period and became extremely popular, spreading via North Africa to the Middle East.

Wednesdays involved visits to the baths and coiffeuses, preparing beauty creams, receiving the latest perfumes from the palace, changing bottles, making toothpicks, and consulting doctors about internal ailments.

On Thursdays between afternoon and evening prayers everyone in the house came to the main room to chant eulogies of the Prophet and recite prayers. The session would begin with a female reciter reading from the Quran. Umm al-Hurr did not allow anyone in the household to miss this occasion unless there was a legitimate excuse.

A particular feature of this noble lady's virtue and experience was that she had seen all the women who worked for her married; the only exceptions were those newcomers who had not yet reached puberty. For that reason she was held in particular affection by the entire group of women who served her, even more so when her husband, the Sultan, had left her some years before his deposition in order to indulge in some fresh pleasures of his own.

CHAPTER SIX

With just a few days remaining from Shamah's required waiting-period Umm al-Hurr was ordered by the Sultan to perform the obligation of the pilgrimage to Mecca. She was permitted to take with her whomever she wished from her female retinue. She chose ten of them, one being Shamah. Two days later the Sultan gave his consent and issued instructions for the company to make ready; it was to carry with it a gift for the ruler of Egypt. A senior member of the Sultan's own entourage was appointed to lead the company.

That night Umm al-Hurr stayed up later than usual. Shamah was at her side, and they spoke about Al-Jawra'i. Umm al-Hurr noticed Shamah's sweetly innocent loyalty to her dead husband. She was still wary about the possible effect on Shamah's sensitive spirit of what she had really wanted to say from the start, but decided to say it anyway. "My daughter," she announced tersely, "God has released you!"

The Sultan permitted his deposed father to travel from his exile in the Western desert to meet his wife as she traveled along the desert route, but he fell seriously ill and died a few days later.

Umm al-Hurr's company took three months to reach Egypt; most of the Maghribi pilgrims that year followed behind. A message had been sent on ahead announcing the imminent arrival of the former consort of the Sultan of Morocco and the Sultan's gift. Over the course of an entire week the company was welcomed at the Egyptian ruler's palace with all due honor and respect. However, some of the Egyptian ruler's imbecile sons blackened their father's name by suggesting to the leader of the Moroccan company that he could further enhance the Sultan's gift by including some of Umm al-Hurr's female entourage. However, the Zanati Judge who was in charge followed Umm al-Hurr's instructions and purchased some female Circassian slaves in the Egyptian market so that her company could continue on its journey to Mecca.

While the company was waiting for a *laissez passer* at the port of `Aydab, it was attacked by a group of masked horsemen who made off with Shamah and one of Umm al-Hurr's maids. However, a Sufi ascetic who had been a disciple of one of the Moroccan shaykhs had given orders to his followers to protect the party while it was passing through his zone of influence. As soon as he heard about the attack, he dispatched his horsemen in every direction. Before sunset on that very same day they brought back the two kidnapped women, having snatched them from the clutches of a group of men who, along with the head of the Egyptian postal service, were taking them to Fustat.*

During the rituals of pilgrimage and penitence Shamah stood alongside her mistress, Umm al-Hurr; in the process she recovered all the spiritual traits that she had acquired in her youth at the side of her other mistress in Salé, Al-Tahirah, wife of Judge Ibn al-Hafid, who had been her companion in ritual-washing and vigils. Left alone, Umm al-Hurr and Shamah spent half the night performing prayers, intercessions, and supplications; half the day was spent circumambulating the Ka'bah and running between Safa' and Marwa. When the time arrived for the pilgrimage rites the tears of devotion shed by the two women transformed them into two kindred spirits poised to shake hands with the angels.

The long trip concluded with a visit to the Prophet's

Fustat: the oldest part of Cairo, to the South of the present-day city (named after *fossata*, the Latin word for a "ditch.")

tomb in Medina. There once again their two spirits blended in the celestial realm of penitence. One morning Umm al-Hurr asked all her female attendants to tell her about the dreams they had had since their arrival in the region of the Holy Places. With Shamah she waited till they were alone together. "After we returned from visiting the tomb of the beloved Prophet," she said, "I fell asleep before sunset and dreamed that you, my lady, were giving me a present, a white horse from Granada." "God willing," replied Umm al-Hurr with a smile, "that will happen!"

On the return journey to the Maghrib the company had reached Sijilmasah when Umm al-Hurr was afflicted with severe pain. Even when they were still in Kinanah territory an Egyptian doctor had already diagnosed the problem as a stomach ulcer. Throughout the trip Umm al-Hurr had been suffering because of changes in water and food, all of which was quite different from what she was used to at the palace. As they approached Jabal Fazaz Umm al-Hurr spent a really bad night. Next morning she summoned the company leader and two jurists, asked them to convey her satisfaction to the Sultan who had looked after her interests, and prayed for his continued felicity. She then gave instructions regarding her sons and daughters, as well as details about the place where she wished to be buried. She specifically asked that the Sultan should respect her wishes regarding her married servant-women who were foreigners by returning them to their families if they so desired. Regarding Shamah in particular, she requested that she should be returned immediately to the care of Judge Ibn al-Hafid in Salé.

No one in the company knew for sure when Umm al-Hurr passed away; they were just about to enter Fez itself. The Sultan came out in person to greet the company, now including her corpse. Ibn al-Mubarak, the leader of the group, stood before the Sultan. Handing him Umm al-Hurr's will with its various requests, he mentioned all her virtuous acts during the journey and in the Holy Places.

The day of Umm al-Hurr's burial saw a big ceremony in Fez. The Sultan used the occasion to pardon all of his deposed father's former retainers. After the Quran and third day intercessions had been recited, the Sultan ordered her will to be carried out to the letter. As part of that process the Judge in Fez wrote to Judge Ibn al-Hafid in Salé consigning Shamah, by the Sultan's command, to the care of his wife, Al-Tahirah. The task of taking Shamah and the letter back to Salé was entrusted to two servants and a maid from the Sultan's palace.

CHAPTER SEVEN

When she got back to Salé, Shamah found Judge Ibn al-Hafid disillusioned; he had lost much of his energy and influence. His beloved wife, Al-Tahirah, had died months earlier after a severe asthma attack, a condition that had dogged her ever since she had left her own region of Tadla for the humid region of Salé on the sea-coast at the estuary of the River Rikrak. With her death her corps of servants had scattered. Al-Khawdah had married Al-`Ajjal, Shamah's father. They had become acquainted when, following Al-Khawdah's return to Salé and Shamah's departure on the ill-fated expedition to the Eastern territories, he would often come and ask her for news of his daughter.

Dahman, Ibn al-Hafid's son, apple of his eye, and great hope of continuing his line, had died in atrocious circumstances. What had happened was that Jarmun, the Governor of Salé, was anxious to destroy his great rival, Judge Ibn al-Hafid, who managed to make use of his learning as a way of lording it over the Governor. Jarmun therefore invited

Dahman to accompany him and the Sultan's uncle as part of a troop of soldiers that was going to collect taxes from the tribes in the region of the River Sabu. When they arrived at a tribal center to collect those taxes, custom had it that the occasion would be used to hold a party every day which would be paid for by the delinquent tribes until such time as their tax obligations were paid off. One of the features of these parties would be horse-races between the army champions and the Governors present. Dahman, Ibn al-Hafid's son, always shone in these contests, leaving everyone else far behind, including the Sultan's elderly uncle. Dahman was so thrilled by the way the women watching cheered at his victory that he forgot that his rivals in the race were high-class people who were extremely aware of their own status, not least the Sultan's own uncle. On the second night of the troop's sojourn with the tribes, Jarmun, the Governor of Salé, managed to persuade some of the soldiers to suggest to the Sultan's uncle that he take fiendish revenge on the upstart from Salé. Dahman found himself invited to dinner in the Prince's tent. Even though he had never drunk wine before, they made him down a lot of it. Too drunk to know what was happening, he was handed over to a group of slaves who subjected him to all sorts of gruesome sport until he died. His corpse was returned to his father in Salé.

After a series of calamities like this, Ibn al-Hafid

no longer bothered himself with Jarmun's intrigues. The Governor continued to acquire more influence for himself at the Judge's expense. He claimed that the Judge had been a close confidant of the former Sultan and his status as a member of the judiciary had not been reconfirmed. However, in spite of all Jarmun's machinations, people continued to flock to see Ibn al-Hafid, to offer him their sympathy, to ask his opinion, to seek his arbitration, and to volunteer to serve him. In any case, the letter that had been sent about Shamah had come straight from the Sultan; it had been addressed to him as Judge of Salé. Its requirements had to be carried out, and a copy had to be sent to Jarmun for filing. The next day, the Judge contacted the inspector of endowments in Salé, requesting that he identify a house for Shamah. The Judge then got the house ready, installed Shamah in it, and designated a monthly allowance for her to be paid by the port inspectorate, all this in spite of opposition from Jarmun.

Two weeks after Shamah had been installed in her new abode, the Judge sent one of his retainers to the mosque between the two evening prayer-times in order to look for a person who used to sit there every day at this particular time. His name was `Ali Sancho. He was the chief mosaic craftsman hired to decorate the religious college that the Sultan had ordered built in Salé; the Sultan had brought him from Andalusia especially for this purpose. However, even though he had been trained by the very best Muslim craftsmen over there, he had remained a Christian until his conversion to Islam was formalized by Judge Ibn al-Hafid two weeks after his arrival (in other words, six months before this particular day). His conversion had been the talk of the town in Salé; the new Muslim had been the focus of attention for all the scholars and preachers of the town. Ever since his conversion, he had never left Ibn al-Hafid's table. He was now devoting all his attention to memorizing some portion of the Quran in addition to the verses that he was so skillfully installing on the walls of the new college. He was determined to learn what was required of a good Muslim.

`Ali Sancho entered the Judge's library and found him consulting commentaries on the subject of deeds by day and night. Once they had exchanged greetings and had a brief chat about the arrival of all the materials needed to decorate the Sultan's new college, the Judge broached with `Ali the topic for which he had invited him, namely a suggestion that he agree to marry a woman named Shamah. He told `Ali that Shamah's story was already well known in Salé; in the wake of her return to the city at the personal command of the Sultan, her tale had become the talk of every mosque. The Judge then went on to explain how he saw things happening. He was ready, he said, to pay the dowry, buy the trousseau, and furnish the house that Shamah was now occupying. He described Shamah's virtuous qualities and the high esteem in which his late wife had held her. He closed by noting that, now God had opened `Ali's heart to Islam, this was a veritable gift from the heavens, part of a plan from the unseen.

`Ali beamed in gratitude and stood up to kiss the Judge's hand. "If Shamah consents and the timing is agreeable to her," the Judge went on, "the dowry will be fixed this coming Friday. I will provide fifty dinars as part of the marriage agreement. Shamah will be able to spend it on her husband as she sees fit until such time as you can repay it."

Once `Ali had left, the Judge spent some time pondering. From his in-laws' household in Salé he selected a maid to serve in Shamah's house and a servant to run errands and guard the door. He then set out for Shamah's house, eager to tell her what he had planned and see what she thought about the marriage. He had sent word ahead that he was on his way along with two brass saucepans with dinner food. He was aware that her father, Al-`Ajjal and his wife, Al-Khawdah, were staying with Shamah during these early days following her return to Salé. The Judge alone sat with Shamah. In order to satisfy his own curiosity and cheer her up, he asked her a host of questions about her husband, Al-Jawra'i, the terrible journey to the Eastern territories, the routines in

Umm al-Hurr's household, and the pilgrimage to Mecca and Medina. When he asked her whether she would consent to the idea of being married to `Ali, she agreed. With tears welling in her eyes, she stood up and kissed the Judge's head. She left the room and came back with Al-Khawdah and her father. The Judge now repeated his suggestion to Shamah regarding the marriage. Her father agreed, as did Al-Khawdah who, returning with Shamah to the kitchen, unleashed trills of delight that were loaded with a mutual understanding between the two women. However the noise was not sufficiently loud to arouse their neighbors' curiosity.

At noon on the following day Al-Khawdah devised a scheme so that Shamah could catch a glimpse of her future husband. It involved visiting the home of a woman whose house was next to the college where `Ali was working. Shamah watched him through an aperture in the wall as he walked around the courtyard or terrace, with just a few feet separating them. When she saw his firm physique, light complexion, blond hair, and blue eyes, she sensed the kind of longing for men that she had not felt since her adolescent years in Ibn al-Hafid's household. She was so afraid someone might see her, she felt compelled to leave; either that or else she had seen all she needed. When she came back to Al-Khawdah, she was panting and almost stumbled; she was so overcome that her knees nearly gave way.

Because of all the trouble caused by the incident involving Shamah and the boiling-hot water, Judge Ibn al-Hafid preferred not to involve any members of his household in Shamah's wedding. There was no fuss. At the banquet, Ibn al-Hafid's companions took turns as usual in reciting literary and judicial anecdotes appropriate to the occasion. Someone alluded to Al-`Ajjal's purported Spanish origins by citing "Birds of a feather flock together," and someone else cited the Quran regarding `Ali's good fortune in spite of his recent conversion to Islam, "These spoils hath He hastened for you." [Surah 48, v. 20] However, since it was Ibn al-Hafid who had supervised `Ali's conversion and sanctioned his marriage to Shamah, the Judge's colleagues showed him respect; indeed they rejoiced with him, invited him to their homes, and gave him gifts.

For reasons well known to the Judge, he declined to sign the marriage certificate himself and asked another Judge to do so. The matter involved a legal uncertainty. Following Al-Khawdah's return to Salé from Fez, the Judge's late wife, Al-Tahirah, had passed on to him some information that she had learned from Al-Khawdah herself. It might well be necessary, she said, to marry Shamah to `Ali as a virgin rather than not.

CHAPTER EIGHT

Once the marriage ceremony had taken place, the guests departed, and `Ali and his bride were now left to celebrate a married life of unprecedented happiness. He discovered that within such a union his new faith would continually intensify. His wife would now be his real counsellor on matters of belief, and he could dispense with all the Muftis in mosques. He need no longer bother his fellow-workers. The two were linked by a secret bond, one that would blossom through love and fidelity, each fostered by fleeting glances. This was a secret known only to Al-Khawdah, and that is why she felt bound to follow the dictates of the situation, using gestures of love, care, and concern. She therefore stayed for seven full days.

At breakfast on their first day together `Ali bashfully asked his bride to make allowances for his Andalusian accent and to overlook some of his old bad habits. He promised to teach her Castilian Spanish.

As time went by, the people of Salé got used to regarding `Ali as a full Muslim; in fact, his fellow-workers noticed a distinct air of spirituality in his countenance. The master-craftsmen were witnesses to his nocturnal devotions, inspirational visions, and revelatory utterances. The arrogance he had initially displayed towards apprentices and servants alike disappeared. They all watched in amazement as he devised entirely new types of mosaic decoration and stucco-carving and suggested to the mosaic craftsman fresh color-patterns that were completely unknown to them. He had similarly inspirational suggestions for the wood-carvers as well. He proposed different types of calligraphy: for Quranic verses that stressed the sublime nature of God he proposed a form emphasizing the vertical, thus drawing attention to themes of might and names that inspired awe; for other verses where the emphasis was on mercy, blessings, delight, and beauty, the calligraphy would emphasize the horizontal and be more slanting. One morning he arrived with a proposal to redo the mosaic for the study-halls and student quarters so as to include three different types of calligraphy representing the essential nature of the religious student: tight patterns to inspire awe in the heart; freer ones to illuminate the unachievable transcendent in God's heavenly gifts; and geometrical ones to reflect the solid foundations of the revealed law. Right angles would be used when needed, and other symmetries would be modeled to suit the thoughts of wise men. Every time word of these ideas of `Ali was reported in various councils, fair-minded people were unanimous in their verdict: this man, for his great sincerity, had been granted a clear revelation from the realm of the unseen, one that was manifest in both his conduct and artistry.

`Ali continued to impress everyone with his copious imaginative powers. After only a few weeks he had completely lost his complex about the way he talked; it was almost as though he had never had any problems with accent and language. That was followed by another period in which he felt a sense of total serenity. Barely uttering a single word, he focused instead on the outlines for the college's mosaics. He poured his whole being into the process, making suggestions to others with an unaccustomed gentleness. He kept at it until he had finished work on the college. It immediately became a model for its exquisite craftsmanship and beauty.

Hardly had the work been completed before the good news was sent to Fez. A senior counselor of the Sultan came to Salé to open the college so that it could receive students, and the Sultan used the same occasion to appoint the college's teachers. Once classes had begun, the master craftsmen, `Ali among them, received gifts from the Sultan. `Ali was authorized by the Sultan's counselor to do mosaic work for any owners of riyads and other mansions in Salé, now that he had married and planned to settle in the city.

CHAPTER NINE

Shamah had been married for a year when work on the Sultan's college came to an end. The Sultan's counselor had barely left Salé before Jarmun, the Governor, started conspiring against ʿAli. His plan involved forcing the inspector of endowments to eject ʿAli from the house where Judge Ibn al-Hafid had put him and preventing the port inspector from paying ʿAli his monthly allowance.

Ibn al-Hafid thwarted every attempt Jarmun made to harm ʿAli Sancho. The vile Governor was by nature someone who felt constrained to suppress all kinds of virtuous conduct. In fact, that is how the people of Salé depicted him. They continually referred to the words of an Andalusian jurist, who, having come to live in the city and heard about the atrocious way the Governor behaved towards the people of Salé, had quoted the Qur'an: "God has poured upon them a punishing whip" [Q. 89.13].

In the fall two years after Shamah's marriage,

Ibn al-Hafid ate some dates and was afflicted by a bad case of diarrhoea. After several weeks in bed a virulent fever took his life, a grievous loss to the city and especially Shamah. Hardly was the Judge buried before Jarmun resumed his intrigues against `Ali. He stopped his allowance and had him ejected from his charity house. `Ali was now forced to rent a misriyyah close to the great mosque. As days went by, it became clear that Jarmun had no intention of restricting his campaign against `Ali to these measures. He now started warning city notables who were eager to hire him as a craftsman not to do so. Such a boycott harmed `Ali, but Shamah reminded him that his faith required a level of patience in the face of adversity. Even so, she too was worried as she contemplated the likelihood of a gloomy future.

`Ali now began to run out of money, but he was unwilling to sell any of Shamah's valuables. When he could find no one ready to defy Jarmun's ban on employing him, he thought about taking Shamah to another city. Just at that point however he met a merchant from Amalfi who used to bring all kinds of Genoese goods to sell at the Oil Hostelry in Salé: textiles, pots and pans, and razors. In exchange he bought wool and walnuts and took them back to the lands of the Christians (as Europe was called in those days).

For centuries this Oil Hostelry in Salé had already

been renowned as a commercial center. It only occupied a few hundred square meters, and the courtyard was only large enough for three large scales, an inn for merchants to stay in, and no more than forty stores. However, it did serve as the headquarters for Salé's commercial tax office. The building was the hub of a commercial district full of stores, restaurants, and inns, where goods were displayed and rooms rented. It was a hive of activity to which people flocked to make deals and arrange for hire-purchase and various types of covert interest. There were money-changers and gossip-mongers. The people involved were a mixture of religions and races, bartering in a variety of languages and doing business with Bedouins and blacks, people from the mountains and cities of the interior, and others from overseas—Algeciras, Livorno, Bijayah,* and elsewhere.

This Amalfi merchant had two shops for storage and displaying wares at the lower end of the Oil Hostelry, with a private room on the top floor. He made an agreement whereby `Ali would manage his commercial affairs in Salé and be his correspondent and deputy. The merchant's partner in Bijayah had just died, and, since he had more business in that port, he preferred to direct things there for himself since it was closer to his own domestic markets and his family home.

Bijayah: (French, Bougie) a port city, now on the coast of Algeria.

So the Amalfi merchant stayed for a month, negotiating deals, opening accounts, getting to know a number of customers, and accustoming himself to the pace of activity in the Oil Hostelry, but then he went on his way, leaving `Ali Sancho to run his business. `Ali took his wife to live in the room on the fourth floor of the Hostelry.

Shamah only took a small amount of furniture to her new abode since the room in the Oil Hostelry was very small. Her only thought was to be near `Ali, as though to protect him from all the plots being hatched against him. It never occurred to her to compare her current lodging, more like a mouse-hole, with the house of Ibn al-Hafid in which she had grown up, with Al-Jawra'i's fabulous residence in Fez, or with Umm al-Hurr's quarters in the Sultan's palace. Throughout these previous changes in her life she had been a body with no heart or will, albeit one kept in boxes of marble and crystal and encrusted with precious stones. But now the fates had smiled on her, and she was living in a firmament of emotion, untrammeled save for the occasional twinge of fear concerning a devoted love in the depths of her heart, one that grew and expanded with every passing day; all of which diverted her attention from worldly activities going on all around her. Here she was living an apparently pre-destined existence, one that blended a total, passionate love with a terrible fear of tyranny and life's calamities. Shamah, beautiful and overflowing with emotions, had been born and raised in a cowherd's tent. She had kept the secrets of palace ladies, shared their anxieties day and night, and learned from them culture in all its variety and the proper way to recite the Quran. She had survived the intrigues of more than one harem, had been married to a man whose every command was obeyed and who possessed all the trappings of prestige. He had taught her to give but not to take. She had experienced the fear of becoming a prisoner, she had learned about life on the battlefront in distant lands, she had seen death, the grim reaper, written on the surface of the sea's clashing waves, she had become the widow of a man whose burial place was still unknown to her, and had been part of an inheritance passed on to Sultans. Fate had protected her against palace slave-traders who bartered reputations and had instead blessed her with the protection of a perfect royal mistress. She had then experienced the rigors of long-distance travel, twice escaping from the clutches of slave-dealers. In the Prophet's own lands she had purged her chiding soul of the sins of others with plentiful tears day and night so as to rise to the highest stations of the soul, she who, ever since her birth, had known only service and deeds of charity and beneficence. She was a power for good, a pure soul, an innocence uncorrupted by the vicissitudes of time.

Within a few days Shamah had grown accustomed to

her new home, the cramped space, the noise, the dirt, and the diverse neighborhood. After everything that had happened to her, she now felt that she was living with her soul-mate; so nothing else mattered. This man, `Ali, was now an essential part of her. Her problem was finding a way to expand the space inside her since as day followed day his spirit was occupying more and more of her emotional make-up.

Those who suggested that Shamah was a gift from heaven for this Muslim man were not mistaken. But what they did not realize was that both of them were essentially reborn, having been rescued from an inferno. With such a past in mind, it did not matter if some vicious or malicious person decided to do them harm; Shamah and `Ali were both existing in some absolute time, one that would envelop and enfold them for ever.

Shamah was prepared to swear also that `Ali carried her within him just as she did him. She knew exactly how to read his book, one that, ever since they had first met, had once again become a blank sheet with no writing on it. Nothing written in a book has any meaning; all learning lies within the way pages fold and conjoin. `Ali's silences were speech, and his alien ways went back to a time before he had gained entry to this safe haven, Shamah's heart. Such magnanimity reminded her of stories that she and the other women in

Ibn al-Hafid's household had heard from a preacher, named Abu `Ishrin, who had read to them from behind a curtain. One day he had talked about the heart. It was not, he said, merely a muscle that pumped blood around the body; it was something invisible, like a niche in a wall containing a lamp that gives off a gentle or gleaming light. People can use this light to read, in other words to understand, what is in the world. She remembered the preacher saying that the niche might grow into a room or a palace reaching to infinity, as an act of thanksgiving to its Creator; it would either revert to Him or else remain in place for ever. As Shamah recalled this occasion with particular vividness, she realized that it was grace that would enlarge her heart and make it a palace of infinite size, one large enough to encompass her life-companion, `Ali. She could not even imagine letting him take her heart with him when he ventured out to the market; after all, had not God given him a wife as a boon and act of mercy so as to provide him with a quiet life! She could scarcely imagine her heart leading an existence separate from his, one that was the bearer of such a mighty faith. For that reason she determined that he was her superior, in that he was the one who had created and crafted her heart, just as he had the decoration for the Sultan's college. It was purely a matter of chance that had brought them together and thus saved her from the clutches of wolves. Now she had been made beautiful for the very person who deserved her. Bolstered by a combination of love and grace her heart would expand for him. Even so, she had the impression that her problem would remain unresolved until she could find a solution to the equation involving him, her, and the Creator. There was however a glimmer of understanding which led her to conclude that any expansion of her heart would involve her in a good deal of sighing and groaning.

These deep thoughts were interrupted when her husband, `Ali, came home. After sitting down he told her the good news that he had just received five loads of Amalfi-made caps and hats which he had been able to sell immediately. The profits were enough to keep him going even if he did not get anything else for several months.

There was a knock on the door, and in came Al-Khawdah to pay her first visit since the couple had moved to the Hostelry. With a single glance she took in the place where they were now living and realized how shabby it was compared with the quarters where Shamah had lived before. That affected her deeply. She put down the things she had brought with her, butter, honey, and nut-shell used as part of make-up, then told them that her husband, Al-`Ajjal, Shamah's father, was feeling better after a cold. She told them that, before her husband had been lost at sea, she had become very familiar with this Hostelry, the people who frequented it, and its various customs. She talked about the golden days of the Hostelry, when the purchasing needs of Ibn al-Hafid's household--utensils, furnishings, and children's items--were all brought to his house by merchants from the Hostelry, especially Jews and Christians who were trusted enough to come to the house and even enter the inner courtyard of the riyad so that they could show the women their wares; this applied especially to Jewish and Christian women who did not have to wear the veil. Muslim parfumiers and jewelers were afforded the same privilege. Al-Khawdah told `Ali that she was personally acquainted with the Amalfi merchant for whom he was acting as agent. It was thanks to Ibn al-Hafid (who had interceded with the Inspector of Markets) that permission had been given to knock down an intervening wall between two rooms he was renting on this floor and thus create the space where Shamah and `Ali were now living.

Shamah was eager to learn as much as she could from her dear friend about the occupants of this commercial establishment. To her it seemed for all the world like a replica of Noah's ark. Just at that moment Shamah spotted through her half-open door one of her neighbors coming towards her on his way back to his own room. He was a tall man with a rosy complexion; he wore shoddy clothes, but they were always clean. He used to carry a basket with him, and lived in the room directly opposite Shamah's. As the two women watched him from the back of `Ali's room, the man closed the door behind him. No sooner had he done so than Al-Khawdah started telling Shamah about him. His name, she said, was Abu Musa; his acquaintances in Salé knew him by his town-name of Tamisna. He was not employed, but he wasn't a beggar either; he managed to live on seaweed. He had been living in a cave by the sea till the Inspector of Markets had brought him to live in this room which was set aside for people like him who wished to live the life of a hermit. The previous occupant had been an eccentric maniac whom people had nicknamed "the megaphone." The weirdest of all the escapades involving him had occurred when he had brought a donkey into the courtyard of the Great Mosque as people were leaving the Friday prayers and started playing with it. Passers-by observed him in total disgust, but other people who would regularly share a joke with him asked why he was behaving this way. "At this very moment," he replied, "I'm repairing the hole in the ship." As was usually the case, people did not take this reply seriously; the man was as irresponsible as a child. However, when some people returned to Salé with news of the fate of the Sultan's own ship, which had managed to avoid the disaster that struck the rest of the fleet on its way back from the Eastern provinces, they told everyone that, battered by fierce winds, their ship had struck a rock and sprung a leak. Water had come pouring through in such profusion that even the most experienced sailors had totally despaired of plugging the hole; to a man they were convinced that everyone would perish. It was just then that they noticed one of their number, a man who looked exactly like the maniac they all knew as "the megaphone," bringing planks, pushing back the water, banging in nails, and plugging the hole with a kind of tar more adhesive than anything they had ever seen in their lives before. At the time no one had even thought about questioning this man or marveling at what he had done; they were all much too worried about saving their own skins. But when some of these men described the incident in detail, the people in Salé recalled a particular day when the maniac had been playing with the donkey in the mosque and the answer he had given them at the time. But, when they went to question him further about the whole thing, they had found him dead in his room.

At this point the water-carrier arrived at his usual time and was admitted to fill up the water-jar in the room. The two women glanced over at `Ali; they had been chatting for so long that he had fallen asleep on the bed.

The two women said their goodbyes, and Al-Khawdah left. A short while later she came back with a young blonde girl in her early teens, named Julia. She was living on the same floor of the Hostelry with her father who was a Christian merchant from the town of Alicante in Andalus. His particular trade was tanning and selling leather goods from Western regions. He had come to Salé from Gibraltar several years ago, bringing his daughter, Julia, with him. Her mother was dead. Julia had learned Arabic and, like her peers, had regularly entered houses in Salé along with a mixed group of boys and girls. She seemed to have spent many days and nights at the homes of Muslim acquaintances, social contacts, and workers known to her father. She had been welcomed in such houses both because of her beauty and her engaging Andalusian accent; in addition, her name, Julia, put the Berbers living in Salé in mind of the word in their language meaning "idiot." However, as Julia became older, she began to rebel against her father's instructions. For his part, he did not like sharing a room with her and was worried about what might happen to her in this land where he was himself living in exile. At the same time he was reluctant to give up all the profits he was making in Salé just so that he could take his daughter back to Spain and her normal Christian environment; even there she would be living among Andalusian Muslims. What scared him more than anything was the thought that the day might come when she would tell him that her friends had finally persuaded her to convert to Islam.

Al-Khawdah now presented Julia to her friend, Shamah. In fact Julia had only known Shamah since her arrival at the Hostelry; she had not been allowed inside Ibn al-Hafid's house.

The three women stood there, partially shielded from the public eye by the balcony that circled the inner courtyard of the Hostelry. Julia immediately told Shamah that she was delighted that Shamah had arrived, since that meant she was no longer the only respectable female resident in the Hostelry. Shamah decided not to inquire further as to what she meant by that statement. Meanwhile Julia proceeded to say that her father, whose name was Pedro, was acquainted with `Ali, Shamah's husband, and admired him greatly. He was anxious to form a close friendship with him, since they both came from the same country and spoke the same language, even though `Ali had decided to change his name after settling in Salé. "The strangest thing about this place," she went on quickly in order to change the subject, " is that there's only one toilet."

CHAPTER TEN

Next day `Ali went down to his shop. He was busy
dealing with requests from some Bedouin customers, when
the tax-collector appeared to discuss the price of the hats he
had sold on the previous day. Every time the man tried to
reckon up the tax due, he was not satisfied with the result; he
kept claiming that the taxable amount on each item was less
than what was due. The argument went on. `Ali realized that
he could not devote himself properly to his customers while
this dispute was going on and that there appeared to be no
immediate end in sight. The atmosphere soon turned heated.
The tax-collector started impugning the merchant's reputation in a way that could only be justified if his real intent was
to insult him directly. Even so, `Ali gritted his teeth and put
up with the tax-collector's insults. However, just then one of
the tax-collector's aides who had been observing things from
a distance stepped up and threatened `Ali for arguing with his
master, something that had to be stopped. Now the argument
between the three men turned into a shoving match. Merchants who had previously been preoccupied with buying and

selling things in the Hostelry began to pay attention to what was going on. One of the merchants came over and gestured to `Ali behind the tax-collector's back. `Ali understood what the man meant. "Just tell me how much I owe you," he told the tax-collector, "and I'll pay you." The tax-collector's reaction was to launch into a hail of vile insults against `Ali, impugning his honor and calling his honesty into question. `Ali now completely lost his temper and started yelling. A second aide now stepped forward. Helped by the first, he tried to grab `Ali and drag him out of the Hostelry. A huge din now ensued as `Ali broke free and pushed one of the tax-collector's aides so hard that he fell flat on his back. The scenario now turned into a battle involving `Ali and the three men, something the Hostelry had rarely witnessed before. It seems that `Ali's yelling eventually made its way up to the fourth floor, since Shamah looked over the balcony railing and was astonished to discover that he was indeed the one making all the noise. Grabbing a shawl and wrapping it round herself, she made her way downstairs as quickly as possible. She tried as best she could to extract her husband from the heat of this battle. All the merchants, customers, and nosey passers-by saw the scene for themselves: an angelic beauty of a woman coming to the aid of a recent convert to Islam who had fallen into the tax-collectors's clutches, he being someone against whose evil ways they all sought refuge in God just as much as they did the Devil's own demons. Just then, three guards who, it appeared, just happened to be passing by the Hostelry, threw themselves on `Ali, handcuffed him, and shoved him out of the Hostelry ahead of them. Meanwhile the tax-collector and his two accomplices insisted on taking this woman with them since she too had taken part in the humiliation of this official of the Sultan.

`Ali and Shamah now found themselves thrown into a prison at Governor Jarmun's headquarters. It consisted of a tiny house where accused people were held to await trial. As the two of them were led through the city markets, the very sight provoked both amazement and disgust, not only because women were never treated this way but also because many of them were well acquainted with the arrested man; they knew him to be a good person and a gifted craftsman whose particular virtues had shown him the light of true faith and led him to the path of forgiveness.

The news spread rapidly through the city. Some worshippers asked the Imam of the great Mosque, a jurisconsult named Bu `Asharah, to intercede on behalf of the wronged man, and he promised to do so after the evening prayer. By that time however `Ali and Shamah had both appeared before the Governor, Jarmun, who had insulted `Ali and ordered Shamah to remove her veil since she had been the one responsible for committing an outrage against one of his blameless employees. After threatening them with further action, he let them go, but only after they had paid a fine equivalent to half the total worth of `Ali's business.

Like two children who have no idea of the real value of money and do not believe that evil exists, `Ali and Shamah, now released from the clutches of Jarmun and his devious machinations, shut the door of their room behind them. For two whole days they surrendered to their dreams. On the third day, there was a knock on their door. It was Pedro the merchant, coming to tell `Ali that boxes of metal utensils and Indian silk cloth had just arrived for him from Genoa. `Ali thanked Pedro, well aware that this fellow-countryman of his had a special affection for him, especially after the dreadful way the tax-collector had treated him. By now word had spread far and wide that the entire episode had been con-cocted by the Governor, and the intended target had been Shamah, not `Ali.

`Ali now went downstairs, accepted his goods, and secured them in his storage-room. He asked people who kept inquiring about sales to wait for a while. Then he went to the market, bought whatever household items he needed, and rejoined Shamah in their home. He gave a detailed de-scription of the goods that had just arrived and pictured for her the kind of solidarity he had sensed in the looks he got from Hostelry merchants who passed by. However, Shamah's response to his impressions came as something of a surprise. "Don't rely on any support from merchants and agents in the Hostelry," she said. "Their hearts are dead, but they're very clever. Before anyone finds himself compelled to confront agents of tyranny, he is bound to lose his mind and recover his heart. It's only a matter of pure chance that you're a merchant. You may not be as crafty as they are, but they still envy you your good fortune. Are you really that lucky?!"

In fact `Ali was well aware that the source of his luck was Shamah; in fact, she was fortune personified. As day followed day she managed to apply her powerful faith to the cause of eradicating at least some small part of the pervasive sense of panic that enveloped him. Every passing hour saw his admiration for her intense pride increase, a pride that filled her soul and to such a degree that it was able to quash all vanity without being part of it. What she had in mind was to rid `Ali's mind of the dire consequences made all the more likely by Jarmun's clear intention to harass both of them as much as possible.

"Let's suppose," she told him, as though revealing the future's secrets, "that Jarmun does wipe out your business, and we're forced to beg; or that he makes you leave the country without me; or that he imprisons you for life and forces me to become a servant in the homes of rogues like him, just in order to provide for you; or that he imprisons both of us and puts chains on our necks; or even that he kills one or other or both of us. He's certainly evil enough. Even so, he would not be able to deprive me of the trust that noble people far more honorable than he have placed in my cultured soul. They used almost to venerate me because I provided a perfect mirror for their own high morals and noble sentiments. Today I despise this person who lords it over the people of Salé, whereas I almost worship you. Everything we can do, whether we manage to gain respect now or later, will simply be a repetition of the way we have lived ever since we met—and we have certainly not reached the end as yet!—and of the profoundest love that we have shared with each other. People who take whatever steps may be necessary to protect themselves from the assaults of tyrants only raise their own importance. Under this particular tyrant's administration there is no hope for the future. However I can recall something that the preacher who used to sit behind the curtain in Judge Ibn al-Hafid's house used to tell us about forbearance: he would term it "politeness to the Creator." But for the time being, let's forget all about this tyrant and the uncharted future. Instead I'll tell you something else about politesse."

`Ali listened to everything Shamah had to say, but only

understood part of it. After all, Shamah had made her way through a variety of palaces. She had steeped herself in the culture of any number of civilizations and served people of truly refined taste and politesse who were well attuned to learning and exquisite forms of expression. Had 'Ali resisted the suggestions that Shamah was making (as he was entitled to do) and decided instead to follow his own basic instincts and desires, he would have rushed down to the sea, looked out over the bluffs, and told it about the things he had heard from Shamah. He would have demanded to know whether what he had heard was correct. The sea, of course, is utterly unconcerned about the future, so it has nothing to fear. By now Shamah's heart had turned into water and reverted to its original form, the one from which every living thing is created. Had she not just told him that the hearts of all the merchants and agents were forever dead?! He had been utterly amazed when they had been led off to prison together and yet had not shed even a single tear. After everything that had happened to them both, he had come to realize that water does not weep; life is never afraid. As Shamah herself put it, weakness comes from a desire for repetition and routine. Otherwise one thing or one occasion can compensate for everything else.

Beyond that, whatever remains should not be such as to divert the intrepid.

CHAPTER ELEVEN

Next morning `Ali went down to his store in the Hostelry. Merchants from Sus paid a good price for all his utensils, while others from Fez took all his silk fabric without any haggling. `Ali actually contemplated relinquishing his share of the profits from the first sale and part of the profits from the second too so that he could retain the capital and give his agent his proper share of the profits. He was planning to send them to Bijayah, using the currency of the Sultan in Fez which was the standard money-unit from the Egyptian border all the way down to the boundaries with the blacks in the far West. As far as `Ali was concerned, the fine that Governor Jarmun had imposed on him in exchange for releasing him from prison was a measure that involved him alone.

`Ali went in search of the tax-collector in order to explain his disposition of the funds he had earned from the sale, but failed to locate him. The man's deputy who used to supervise the use of scales in the middle of the Hostelry refused to go through the usual accounting procedure. As `Ali made his way upstairs again, another of the tax-collector's assistants started harassing him. He demanded to see the statement on which the amount of tax owed had been calculated. `Ali showed him not only that, but also the amount paid by the porters who had brought the goods in through the city-gates. This particular tax-collector warned `Ali against any further attempts at fraud. Hardly had `Ali presented him with a sheet detailing all the morning's transactions before the man lost his temper and started yelling at `Ali. "Are you trying to make a fool of me, you lying Christian?!" he shouted. "Didn't you learn your lesson last time? Are you trying to get me into trouble with my boss?"

Hearing the commotion a Bedouin merchant and Jewish agent who were eating their lunch in a corner of the Hostelry came over and intervened in the dispute. Once they had calmed the tax-collector down, they took him off to the storeroom and offered him some chilled Masmudah fruit cocktail in an exquisite cup made of Malaga porcelain with an embossed lip. He started chatting with the two men, and that seemed to make him forget his row with `Ali. It looked as though the entire episode had been concocted. However, when the tax-collector got up to leave, he told the two men, "You're both guarantors of your Christian colleague's good behavior and the amount of tax he still owes. According to the records I have from the authorities at the city-gates, the amounts he brought in are fully a third more than he has recorded. From what his Sus and Fez customers told me when they left the Hostelry, the prices he charged for the goods is significantly higher than what he reported to me. As a result he owes me tax on the unreported excess income he made along with a fine for fraud payable to His Excellency the Governor. As his guarantors, you two must come up with the requisite amount for him before sunset today."

The two men now realized to their horror that, far from having succeeded in calming the tax-collector down and reconciling him with their colleague, `Ali, they were now themselves embroiled in his affairs. In particular, the Jewish agent, someone who had spent his entire life working in the Hostelry, most especially among local merchants and others from the further reaches of desert and sea, almost went out of his mind. He had witnessed all the tricks used by tax-collectors and agents, and the various methods they used to ruin and bankrupt crooked and honest folk alike. Barely had the tax-collector finished speaking before the agent was envisaging the direst of conclusions. He started begging for relief, almost as though he were about to be imprisoned himself.

`Ali was still standing by the bottom of the stairs in the Hostelry waiting for the tax-collector to emerge. When he saw him come out, heard what he had to say to his two colleagues, and noticed how panicked the Jewish agent was, he rushed over to them. "I will definitely pay whatever tax and fines the tax-collector's deputy demands," he said. "May God repay you well, my noble friends, for your kind gesture."

Once `Ali had paid everything demanded of him, he discovered that he had actually lost all his profits and one third of his capital. He returned home to Shamah.

"I heard everything he threatened you with," she said, anticipating what he might say, "and I know he took all the money. As I told you before, that doesn't matter, nor what will happen later. Are you hungry? Would you like some almond juice? Would you like me to entertain you for a while so you can get some sleep?"

Following this second calamity `Ali realized that his wife, Shamah, a woman of the subtlest of emotions and an acute sensitivity, whose tender feelings were enough to embrace every child in the city, was herself like an immovable mountain. So strong was her faith that it would protect her against every onslaught, whether it involved actual physical harm or humiliation. Even so `Ali was still wracked by the same doubts that had afflicted him before and now came back to haunt him once again. He wondered whether in fact Shamah was prepared to stand by him and endure all the outrages that the Governor and his tax-collector were inflicting on them. After all, she was fully aware of being the primary cause of it all. She was ravishingly beautiful, possessed many skills, and knew all the politesses of the most elevated households. She had been the protégée of Ibn al-Hafid, Governor Jarmun's arch-rival. Furthermore, she had been married in a rush to a new convert to Islam and was known to worship him to the point of sheer adoration. Beyond all that, there was a defiant streak to her, something that had manifested itself when she appeared before the Governor without flinching or begging for mercy. At this point `Ali dearly wished that Shamah did not possess all those other qualities that made her so attractive, apart, of course, for her love for him. To tell the truth, he could see nothing to be jealous of other than that wonderful love. If Shamah had been just some ordinary woman married to an ordinary man like him, their love for each other would not have aroused such a degree of capricious envy. Shamah was simply the daughter of a woman of the mountains who through birth and nursing had bestowed on her all the energy she possessed but who had then died during a second childbirth. Shamah was the daughter of a cowherd, someone who had worked for one of the town's luminaries. There was something wrong about a situation in which women from deprived households could present the world with beautiful daughters who could not be protected by wealth and prestige. However, Shamah's attractions did not just lie in her wonderful posture and the fact that she was endowed with every imaginable angelic quality. Those qualities were further enhanced by her innocence and pure soul. To `Ali all of this was manifested in the form of a tranquility like some God-given revelation, something that could transport him to new heights from where he himself could fully feel, taste, and comprehend. By this time he had turned into a different person. How could he possibly imagine his blessings with Shamah in the same breath as with the rest of the world? The truth was that the world envied him. The vile Governor and his insolent tax-collector were both merely fangs and claws from the corporeal world, that grotesque ghoul. Seen in such a light, Shamah was not of this world at all, but of its very antithesis, the world to come. That is why she never cried. How can the world to come cry over this ephemeral dwelling-place? Now `Ali understood what well-wishers at his wedding had meant when they had said: "This he has hastened to you" (Q. 48.20), but he had had no idea that everything Shamah meant to him and other people, everything she was bestowing upon him, was simply an advance on something yet more amazing and precious. Were he to be offered yet more, he was not sure he could imagine or even bear it. Yet Shamah surely had even more to offer. He could not yet claim to have discovered every aspect of her treasured gifts, but he was still convinced that from her very soul she was giving him things that his own feeble heart could not comprehend. Every day he found himself wasting so much of the gift she was giving him, and all through his own weakness. Yet the source never dried up. He came to appreciate that the person with a truer love is the one with a bigger heart; from it love flows towards the beloved. Our misery is caused not only by other people's miserly behavior, but also, and especially, by our own inability to accept gifts when they are offered.

He was amazed to realize that all this understanding was manifesting itself to him at this particular time. Casting a glance at the corner of the room, he spotted a jar full of Meknes oil, a present from a former student of his who did plaster carving. He decided to ask Shamah to make a bean paste using this oil and spices, just as it had been made for workers in Ibn al-Hafid's household when he had been working on the Sultan's college. He felt sure that Shamah would be able to give a special touch to such a plebeian dish.

He then invited Pedro and his daughter to share the dish with them. Once they had all finished, `Ali and Pedro went over to a corner and started chatting by the light of a lamp. Shamah and Julia meanwhile sat in another corner and exchanged gossip by the light of a gently flickering candle. Shamah listened as Julia talked about herself. Shamah realized that this teenage girl was going through all the normal problems of someone of her age and needed someone to offer her advice and comfort. Every so often, Shamah would look over at the two men. They were deep in serious conversation, their voices lowered. Even so, she managed to pick up a smattering of what was being said and realized full well what it was that her husband was discussing with his guest.

`Ali told Pedro about the second incident with the tax-collector that day, the way he had been harassed and the fines that had been imposed on him. At the time Pedro had been down at the port on some business of his own. `Ali then got to the point: he was absolutely convinced, and so was Shamah, that the tax-collector had been operating on the Governor's orders. Jarmun was hell-bent on causing him as much grief as possible. He would not allow him to pursue his trade in the Hostelry; in fact he would be using every means at his disposal to break him. For that very reason he had decided to ask Pedro to take over his business, by putting him in charge of receiving goods from his agent in Amalfi who had by now moved his own business to Bijayah.

Pedro agreed to split half the profits with `Ali while the other half remained the property of the agent who owned the capital. With the first caravan that left Salé for Sabtah `Ali sent a letter to his agent in Bijayah informing him of the measures he had been forced to take and the reasons why he had made such a decision. He requested that in future all consignments, whether by land or sea, should be sent in Pedro's name, it being recognized all the while that `Ali would remain the guarantor of the capital. The Amalfi agent in Bijayah was asked to notify all his correspondents in the Northern Mediterranean, the Central Maghrib, and Africa of the arrangements.

Over the course of a month two consignments arrived in `Ali's name, but he did not put in an appearance on the trading floor in the Hostelry. Instead he gave Pedro the task of receiving the goods, storing them and trading in accordance with the terms on which the two men had agreed. Everything seemed to be going according to plan. But then one day, as `Ali was returning home from evening prayer in the Grand Mosque where he would attend a class almost every day after the prayer, two of the Governor's aides were lying in wait for him by the Hostelry door. They summoned him to appear before the Governor. He asked them to wait while he informed Shamah, but they refused on the grounds that she was already aware of their coming because they had knocked on the door a short while before.

The two aides took `Ali away and shoved him into the Governor's jail-cell, in other words the disgusting room known as the "bunayqa". There he spent his first night away from Shamah since they had been married. He wept at the thought, his heart torn by anguish at the thought of being so unjustly treated. But then he thought of Shamah who would be taking the whole thing bravely and steadfastly; that helped calm him down. However it was not long before he started worrying again. He wanted her to be weeping over his fate, but this mood soon changed once he realized that she too might have been subjected to who knows what kind of treatment. Perhaps she had been forced to spend the night away from their room, some place where she might have to confront all kinds of intrigue. At that point he recalled her great love, her defiance, and her worthiness of all the confidence that he put in her. Finally he realized quite how fragile all these noble sentiments and lofty traits were in the face of the sheer power of corruption and tyranny.

`Ali was so overcome with fear, hunger, cold, and paranoia that he spent the entire night wide-awake. When the voices of various muezzins announced the dawn call to prayer, he heard the sounds echoing through an aperture in the Bunayqah. He told himself that, even if Shamah herself had managed to get any sleep, by now she would be in her prayer-space as usual. She would be praying for him, and her prayers could penetrate the very heavens. His new faith, he realized, just like his old one, balanced the boons of life with its miseries, that being a topic that preachers had often broached during the times he had spent sitting with them in the Grand Mosque.

Next day `Ali was taken from his prison-cell and brought before the Governor. He was accused of trying to corrupt the city's merchants, those of the Hostelry in particular, since merchants from distant lands had written to him asking him to divert their custom to other trading-posts. `Ali denied the charge, but the Governor first silenced him and then swore at him. He proceeded to issue a series of threats against `Ali, stating that, if he repeated the offence for which he was being charged, he would be subjected to a colossal and unprecedented fine which would involve making up for all the losses suffered by the Sultan's tax-authorities for an entire year.

`Ali was now released and returned to his home at the Hostelry. Shamah greeted him with showers of affection, but without saying a word. As her anxiety subsided little by little, she managed to ask him what had happened, and he gave her his account. She listened without comment, almost as though she knew it all in advance or anticipated what he would have to tell her; either that, or else she could comprehend the unseen writ large but not grasp the smaller details or be particularly bothered with them.

CHAPTER TWELVE

At this particular point in time all the merchants in the Hostelry were subjected to a process of reassessment, and in every case the rent was increased. Some of the merchants were unable to meet the new demands because, on order from the Governor himself, the market-inspector got some bogus bidders to raise the stakes. The purpose behind it all, people said, was to force a Bedouin who lived on the fourth floor to vacate the premises; he usually set up his stall outside the Hostelry and sold thyme, baked beans, and henna. In fact, he did leave, and his place was taken by a woman in her forties named Tudah. So renowned was she for her cantankerous moods and for always stirring up trouble that everyone called her "the pest." She had a vile reputation, and was apparently connected with the Governor in some way. Rumor had it that he had selected her to take the place of the Judge's assistant who had turned old and senile.

Shamah immediately realized that this woman's proximity augured nothing but bad. It took only a few days for her behavior to become obvious. She would start singing brazenly, lean out of the upper windows, and yell down to the residents, merchants and customers. She would leave the door of her room wide open and lounge in front of it in every kind of posture, not caring in the slightest about anyone. Strangers visiting the Hostelry were welcomed into her room without hesitation. But what bothered Shamah the most was that this Tudah the Pest was totally brainwashing Julia, Pedro's daughter. Julia started frequenting her room, and the two of them would start cackling and whispering. This process involved distancing herself from Shamah, but Julia was not satisfied just to do that; she lied to her father and claimed that Shamah was tempting her to convert to Islam.

The fact of the matter is that Shamah was one of those people who by temperament will automatically shoulder other people's burdens. As a result she naturally felt impelled to take this strange young girl under her wing, a girl in the prime of her youth who was living with her father in a single room. Shamah was one of that rare breed of people who feel an altruistic sense of responsibility for the world around them, just like one of its prophets. This was particularly so when a case of fraud needed to be resolved, a wrong to be righted, or a weakness to be sympathetically handled. None of this was based on any superhuman competence that she possessed, but simply on an instinctive sense that resided deep inside her soul. Her motivation involved the voluntary offering of a self that found in self-sacrifice and effort not merely a source of pleasure but a reason for living.

Now here was this flippant woman, Tudah, coming between Shamah and Julia. Indeed, as day followed day, Tudah was training Julia how to defy her own father. The two women would go out to the baths together and attend soirées with people who were not renowned for their sense of probity. It was only a matter of days before disaster struck, when Julia strayed from the straight and narrow. Tudah the Pest was the one at fault. She took Julia out with her on a promenade to the water-reservoirs along with a group of young folk. Once they got there, Julia was manhandled by some spoiled sons of the city's gentry and disappeared with a group of them for quite a while. Her father, Pedro, only found out about it two weeks later, during which time it was generally assumed she had been lost somewhere. Pedro almost went out of his mind from worry. A few days later the Governor sent someone to summon Pedro and informed him that his daughter was at the home of a family whose son stood accused of having raped Julia. Even so, Pedro was only allowed to see his daughter after receiving the governor's permission. He was notified that the Governor was currently in the process of investigating the entire matter. Once Pedro had seen his daughter, who by this time was beginning to recover from her dreadful experience, he was informed that the Governor had not yet completed his inquiries, and so the girl would have to stay where she was until he permitted her to leave. Pedro would be allowed to see her once a week, no more.

Pedro burst into tears and returned sadly home. He was beset by worries that sapped at his mind and body. The only help and comfort he found was with his neighbors, `Ali and Shamah, both of whom he considered utterly honest. `Ali noticed that for the first time Shamah too had cried, not because of the personal calamities that `Ali and she were facing, but rather because of the misfortunes visited upon their friend by his daughter's behavior. Maybe Shamah herself was shocked to realize that the entire life of a woman had been utterly destroyed. However it was Shamah's view that, now that the evil deed had been done, there was no point in dwelling on the villainy of the people who had kept it quiet for so long. Beyond that, she did not dare explain to Pedro what she realized were the real reasons for keeping his daughter until she was cured and exactly how long it would take to wrap things up. She could hardly bring herself to imagine what kind of price the Governor would be extracting from the family of the offender. Her sense of propriety also told her that she should not explain things to `Ali either, since in her view this crime against Julia was an enormous embarrassment for everyone. Shamah was one of those people who did not believe that a sense of shame disappeared when one got married. After all, wasn't that sense of propriety directly linked to one's estimation for the person whom you did not wish to embarrass? She was anxious not to relax her standards on that score and made every effort to protect her husband from the realities of evil tongues and faulty bodily functions. There were times when her secretive behavior almost made her feel as if he were a stranger. But, when she allowed her feelings and emotions to have free rein, she was well aware of the best ways of getting her due share of his attention. In all this she was following the counsel of the preacher who from behind a curtain had talked to the women at Ibn al-Hafid's household. Apart from that, she knew quite enough about flirting to raise herself above the need for baser pleasures.

At this point Tudah the Pest made a point of flaunting herself in front of Pedro as she conversed with the soldiers and guards, just in case he got the idea of doing her some harm since she had been the one who had perverted his daughter with such evil notions. Once a week Pedro would visit the offender's house to see his daughter, although she never said a word in front of him. Two weeks later he was allowed to return and take his daughter away with him. When he arrived, he found that she had grown pale and completely lost her usual rosy complexion. It was almost as if she had suffered a severe hemorrhage or had been cruelly tortured, and the traces were still visible in the blue rings that encircled her listless eyes. When Pedro set eyes on her, he burst into tears. He wondered how all this could have happened to her: what dreadful treatment had she suffered, what vile cocktails had she been forced to drink, and what dastardly crime had been committed against her.

Pedro took her back to the Hostelry, and Shamah started taking care of her, all the while suppressing the anger she felt. For her part Julia felt uncomfortable with Shamah's attentions. From the outset Shamah had plied her with advice and moral instruction, whereas Tudah had opened the flood-gates to Julia's wilder desires and imagination. In fact, Shamah had done all this out of a sense of sympathy for Pedro, Julia's poor shattered father, and as a sign of her own innate goodness. So full of concern and affection was Shamah that Julia gradually warmed to her; every so often they would embrace each other, and Julia would collapse sobbing into her bosom.

Pedro was too devastated to go down to the Hostelry and ply his business; by now his daughter's fate was too well known. Right at this juncture a message arrived for `Ali from the Amalfi merchant in Bijayah, stating that the merchant was giving up all claims on the remaining capital since he had decided to close his operation in Salé. `Ali was delegated to utilize the shop as he saw fit, to pass it on to someone else, or to return the keys to the market-inspector in charge of property.

Julia meanwhile began to regain her strength, although only a portion of her former youthful bloom returned with it. Once again she attached herself to Tudah the Pest and followed her lead, a decision that made Shamah decide to cut her off completely. All this made Pedro deeply unhappy. Here was his daughter behaving like someone who had either lost everything or else was getting involved in things whose dire consequences she did not even realize. It was as if her only response was an instinctive urge to take vengeance on the entire world and rebel against all conventions. She started going out with the Pest without telling her father where she was going. Indeed she went so far as to ask her father to rent her a room of her own. As a threat she told him that, if he didn't do so, she would marry a Muslim. Truth to tell, this threat had no effect on Pedro, since he never regarded the possibility of her marrying a Muslim as a disaster. What stuck in his craw was the feeling that he had now lost his only daughter and had failed to take proper care of her; also that they had been treated so unjustly by the Governor. But as far as religious affiliation was concerned, he never once felt the slightest hatred for his friend, Sancho, Shamah's husband, who had converted to Islam. In his view all religions had their devout adherents; if they decided to convert from one religion to another, it merely meant that they were impelled by a quest for something that they themselves had not found previously. It certainly did not imply that the missing element was not to be found in their previous religion. Anyone who converted to another faith brought their own piety with them, something that worked to the advantage of all religions.

One evening dinner was being served, but Julia had not yet returned to her home in the Hostelry. Pedro went to visit `Ali and Shamah and told them about his problem. The three of them were well aware that Tudah the Pest was already at home. Shamah served the two men walnuts and dried fruit brought from the oases. `Ali made every effort to cheer up his friend and encourage him to resume his business at the Amalfi stand in the Hostelry. He told him not to bother about all the rumors and innuendos that people kept spreading. But Pedro would not give his friend any kind of undertaking that he would accept his advice. Instead he told Shamah that she was wonderful and deserved everyone's love. With that he wished them both farewell and left.

CHAPTER THIRTEEN.

Next day Julia came home at noon-time. She found the door to the Hostelry room open but her father was not to be found. She went to ask Shamah about him, but she refused to answer the girl's question or even to look at her. When Pedro failed to come home that evening, Julia started asking everyone she met in case one of the neighbors knew where he was.

Tudah was not at home to help her search or even to give her a slice of bread. When it got dark, Julia began to feel scared. She started to weep because she was very hungry and realized that she would have to spend the night in an unlocked room. She went back to Shamah. This time, Shamah understood the situation Julia was facing and allowed her to come in. Perhaps, Shamah surmised, her father had been delayed at some market outside the city, had reached the city gates after they had been closed for the night, and had been forced to spend the night in a neighboring village; or else he had been forced to take refuge in a hermit lodge where he would be looked after by the residents, people who would not ask any lodger where they came from or what their religion was.

`Ali returned from his session at the mosque between the two evening prayers and was astonished to find Julia in his home. Shamah told him that Pedro had not returned home and had left the door open. `Ali thought for a moment and then remembered Pedro's last words to Shamah: "You are wonderful, someone who deserves everyone's love." He tried to avoid coming to the obvious conclusion that Pedro had departed and would not be coming back. After eating his dinner, `Ali went to sleep in Pedro's room and left Shamah and Julia in his own.

Next evening Tudah managed to entice Pedro's daughter back to her room. She told Julia that people in touch with the head of the border police had let her know that Julia's father had completed all the transit procedures at the River Sabu crossing; with a knapsack on his back, he had then joined a caravan heading for Sabtah.

With that Julia broke down and wept bitter tears, but Tudah hastened to tell her about the plans she had for her. From now on, she, Tudah, would be mother and father to her; she was well connected with the authorities and could easily protect her. The first of these claims was instantly confirmed when Tudah had words with the relevant officials, as a result of which the market inspector received an order to substitute Julia's name for that of her father as renter of the room of the Hostelry.

As news of this spread, Shamah had all the confirmation she needed of the grim future that lay in store for the Hostelry and its inhabitants. From now on, she shunned both Julia and her protectress, Tudah, and decided to shut her door in their faces.

CHAPTER FOURTEEN

At about the same time the pilgrim caravan on its way
back from Mecca reached Salé. As usual, their arrival was
celebrated by sending a greeting party out through the East
gate in the direction of Tafilalet. The families of the returning pilgrims all took part in the celebration, along with former
pilgrims, members of the nobility, senior religious scholars,
teachers and memorizers of the Quran, children from Quran
schools, ascetics, heads of charities, cantors, anyone in fact
who had good reason to congratulate the returning men and
women who had traversed vast desert wastes and under-
gone severe trials in order to fulfill the solemn obligation of
the pilgrimage and participation in the rituals of the Holy
Places. Everyone in the pilgrimage party was accorded an
initial welcome in the Grand Mosque. Notables and donors
of charity had already sent the choicest products of neighboring villages, foods and other gifts, as donations to needy
pilgrims, along with clothing for any who needed it. After
that, the party broke up, and every pilgrim was taken home
where he was given a special welcome either there or at the

house of a relative or close friend.

During the reception in the Grand Mosque, one of the pilgrims happened to mention that, while he was performing the circumambulation of the Ka`bah and other rituals, he had spotted one of the tenants of the Oil Hostelry, namely Abu Musa. More than one other person supported his account. They then argued with the people welcoming them back as to whether the story could be true or not. Some people said it could not be true because Abu Musa had not left the Hostelry during the pilgrimage season. Even if he had, it would only have been to do what he normally did, namely seclude himself in his cave beside the sea to the North of Salé, spend two or three days there, and then return to town. These doubters scoffed at the people who were claiming to have seen him in Mecca; by way of explanation, they said that, for everyone born, there are forty look-alikes.

Word of this story reached the Governor's ears: that this unknown, strange character called Abu Musa who lived part of the time in the Oil Hostelry and the rest in a cave to the North of Salé, had participated in the pilgrimage this year; that people had actually seen him, encountered him, and even spoken to him during the course of the ceremonies. The Governor sent some of his detectives to check with the city police and especially the guards at the Oil Hostelry, prime amongst whom was the doorman named Abu Ja`rah. Had this Abu Musa been absent long enough, they asked, to perform the pilgrimage to the Hijaz in Arabia. All the answers came back negative. The man's movements from the Oil Hostelry to the cave by the sea had all taken place during the hours that the watch was on duty at the gates.

The Governor now dispatched his Chief of Police to gather witnesses who had actually heard pilgrims specified by name state that they had seen Abu Musa during the pilgrimage ceremonies. After considerable effort the Chief of Police managed to gather twelve witnesses to testify against three of the pilgrims. With regard to the rest of the pilgrim party, he had no luck.

The three pilgrims were now interrogated. One of them confirmed exactly what the witnesses had testified. The two others expressed doubts that the person they met was actually Abu Musa; it was someone very like him, but not the man himself. The two doubters were released on payment of a fine for spreading a rumor that had stirred up so much controversy. The third man was condemned to thirty lashes as a lesson, provided he repented of this flagrant disturbance of the peace. But then the Governor came up with another idea, one that would bolster his verdict against the pilgrim with a written opinion from the senior Mufti in the city. He had no doubt in his mind that the opinion would be in his favor. With that the Governor's name would for the first time be recorded as being someone who had consulted religious scholars on such a peculiar matter as a way of safeguarding the faith, preserving the honor of the witness process, and neutralizing the charge that the Governor acted despotically.

As a result the Mufti, named Yahya Qawlan, received the following request from the Governor:

Be apprised—may God preserve you!—that this year a certain man went on the pilgrimage and returned to his native city of Salé. Witnesses have testified to the fact that this man claims to have met another person during the ceremonies of the pilgrimage, identified him by name, and even spoken to him. However a large number of people in Salé have testified that the man who is supposed to have been on the pilgrimage only left Salé for a matter of hours or days to carry out some simple task outside the city walls. The man against whom people have testified is trying to claim that this other man may have made one of those instant journeys such as are reported from olden times and are attributed to certain holy men. You are requested to give a legal opinion on two matters: is it feasible for one person to be in two places far distant from each other at the same time; and, assuming that this type of instant journey is to be acknowledged, can it be legally recognized and used as a basis for making judgments?

The Mufti sent the following reply:

Be apprised—may God protect His servants—that legal determinations cannot be made on the basis of the assertion of the possibility of someone being in two widely distant places at once. As for instant travel, whether through air or by other means, such things may occur through the spirit or indeed through the body as is well testified for holy men in days gone by; in other words, before the present times when we witness all kinds of evil behavior and flagrant offense.

This fatwa reached Governor Jarmun's residence and was read out to him. He consulted some of his advisers and was informed about its dangerous political implications. In a fury he summoned the Mufti. When the Mufti arrived, he found the Governor surrounded by a number of his retainers, among them the Chief of Police, the Market Inspector, and various cronies who made a pretense of legal expertise. Once the Mufti had presented his greetings, he was allowed to sit. The Governor did not even allow him to get settled before tackling him on the subject: "Qawlan," he said, "here we thought well of you and asked for your opinion, and now you have gotten us in a mess. What is more, you're in the selfsame mess. You have ignored the favors we have bestowed on you and contradicted the precedents of our ancestors. This city must be rid of you before you besmirch it any further. What can possibly have led you to falsify reality to such an extent in your vile document? How can you have brought yourself to insult our mighty Sultan by saying that his era is worse than those of his forebears, characterized by "all kinds of evil behavior and flagrant offense"?

The Mufti was taken aback. His face turned pale, and he started stuttering; the shock of this accusation had taken him completely by surprise. However, bit by bit he recovered his equilibrium and plucked up some courage. "My lord," he responded, "heaven forbid that my choice of words should be thought to impugn the reign of Our Lord the Sultan! What I meant by using the phrase "present times" was a reference to those people who, by defying his regime, choose to disavow his counsel and cast aspersions on his beneficent reign. By no means did I imply those folk who work for the best interests of his people by adhering to the laws of God Almighty.

The Governor interrupted him, turning to one of his coterie who was versed in the law. "So, my legal friend," he demanded, "what do you think of this response?"

"Yes indeed, bountiful provider of mercy and noble deeds," the other man replied with an opinion that seemed both planned and ready, "having now perused the Mufti's response in accordance with your command, I have concluded that the way to get both us and him out of this difficult situation is to establish clearly that this particular opinion in which two specific words (Qawlan) have been utilized"—and here all the courtiers guffawed at the pun on the Mufti's own name, after which the legal authority continued, "to establish that either his opinion implies a severe and calumnious criticism of the current regime in Fez, one that will cause us all grief if it ever reaches the Sultan's ear—that being the interpretation that Your Excellency has put on it; either that or else that, as he himself has now explained, it only involves certain officials and not everyone, in which case the era of Our Lord and Master the Sultan—one in which he has used his lofty status, noble intentions and concern for the welfare of the indigent and for meritorious deeds—will be more worthy than any of its precedents for the manifestation of wonders and for holy men and ascetics to luxuriate in the shade of his beneficence. May God preserve him, he is himself prime among ascetics and noblest of the righteous. As the saying goes, people adhere to the religion of their rulers."

With that, the Governor turned to the Mufti. "We forgive you," he said, "for your opinion, in order to preserve both you and Our Lord, the Sultan's people from the impact of your errors. From now on, do not leave your house."

The Governor next turned to the Chief of Police. "Don't whip the pilgrim who claims to have seen this lunatic. But keep pressing him till he agrees to express some doubts. Then you can let him go."

Finally the Governor spoke to his legal courtier. "Get all the Muftis together—apart from this idiot, and produce a document that reflects what you've just said here. Then we can be rid of this whole matter. Read the text in the mosque, and make sure that the entire affair is framed in ambiguity. Lastly, if anyone dares approach that lunatic or shows any sign of believing him, threaten him with our guards."

The Governor's orders were carried out. Even so, word of what had happened inevitably reached people's ears, and that made them hate the Governor's scheming and tyranny even more. The entire affair drew their attention to this crazy figure, Abu Musa, around whom the whole thing had revolved without him even being aware, consulted, or questioned. He hardly ever spoke to anyone, except to greet people or return salutations. And why should he, when he lived on seaweed? No one had any idea what he carried in the basket that was always with him as he went to and fro. All he ever wore were clothes given to him by people who knew that he never begged. While he was out, they would leave them for him on the washing slab outside his room. He did not seem to use lamps very much at night, whether in his room in the Oil Hostelry or in his cave by the sea. No one dared ask him for anything. People were in awe of him, someone with neither power nor position. Whenever anyone ran into him or spoke to him, he would reply with a pleasant smile that revealed a set of gleaming and flawless white teeth; all this in a small mouth topped by a trimmed moustache and enveloped in a bushy beard without a trace of white in it. He was of average height and sported a pony-tail. His turban, either green or white, was always clean and trailed down at the back. In winter he would wear woolen rags underneath his outer garment; in summer he would put on a woven loin-cloth.

Some women and children started lying in wait to greet him and kiss his hand, but he would avoid that. In fact, for several days he actually disappeared from the city so as to make people aware that he did not like attracting attention.

CHAPTER FIFTEEN

As far as Shamah was concerned, this issue over Abu Musa brought to mind all the stories she had heard about holy men, saints, and people possessed. She talked to `Ali about it with a great deal of conviction. What amazed her in particular was there were two special neighbors of hers that she had not paid any attention to for ages in spite of the fact that both had made a good impression on her from the outset. One was Abu Musa himself, and the second was an old stork that used to squat on an ancient nest at the very top of a willow tree in the center of the Hostelry. This tree, with its gnarled roots and trunk, would spread its leaves all the way from its base up to the fourth floor of the Hostelry. Centuries ago, the ancestors of this stork had constructed a nest right at the point where the branches began to spread out. Shamah had known all about this stork from the time when she was in Ibn al-Hafid's household. Never had she imagined that the day would come when she would be its neighbor. Its story was well-known throughout the Maghrib and in other regions from which merchants would come to

Salé. The stork even commanded a place in the records of the supervisor of endowments because a lady of high rank had stipulated in her will that the revenue from two stores she owned in the butchers' market should be put in a fund to be utilized for the stork's needs; the money was to be used to buy seeds, eggs, and anything else that it seemed to like and want, most particularly when he was looking after a set of chicks and their mother. Older folk said that in times gone by this endowment had also allowed for extra payments to be made to doctors who would treat storks with broken wings and other varieties of damaged birds, in accordance with a fatwa that a Mufti had devoted to the subject. At the beginning of each generation this fortunate stork would bring a female to the nest. There she would breed and hatch her eggs, then leave. The young chicks would grow, and then they too would depart. When the old male eventually died, it never took long for a new stork to take over the nest. Everyone assumed that this new arrival was from the same lineage rather than some other; almost as though it possessed a kind of noble status among the stork species. Things went so far that some folks attributed this form of distinction to the fact that night and day the birds lifted their voices in praise to the Lord. Their very name in Arabic, *laqlaq*, was derived from the phrase *"lak-lak"* (to You, to You), an abbreviation of such phrases as "Praise be to You," "Thanks be to You," and so on. The endowment was still in place, and people continued to weave all kinds of stories around the old bird in the Oil Hostelry in Salé.

Shamah remembered all these stories the way she had heard them as a girl. When she thought about the fate of the female stork, the originator of this proud lineage, her mood changed somewhat. Each female would spend a short time on the nest, give birth, then leave. She thought about the egg which might fall out of the nest and crash to the ground. She also thought about the fact that, because of all the misfortunes that had struck her, she too had not given birth as yet. She dearly wanted a child, but felt anxious and fearful for it. Then the craving for a child came back again, and she felt her stomach churn. Eventually she started calming down, but not before a shiver went right through her just like a pebble that creates ripples across a pond. She took another look at the stork, sitting there on its nest and clearly visible over the top of the floor's balcony. Sometimes it sat serenely on the nest; at others it flapped its wings, creating a clacking noise that reflected all the aches and pains of old age. At this point, Shamah recalled the occasion of her marriage to Al-Jawra'i outside the walls of Salé. She remembered "Warqa'" and the Judge reciting a poem about her to the old folk. She recalled how, while thinking about her, he had come up with the words for the bird and its poetic confidences before giving her a new name, "Warqa'", the name she had adopted for herself, then abandoned—the title of a lovely dream that the Sultan's confidant had concocted for himself. Shamah made a point of not comparing those days gone by with the life she was now living. She was much happier now, wasn't she? There was no need to reflect or compare. Now she could give and take. All kinds of intrigue might be swirling around her, and she was being made to suffer; and yet she was in love and knew full well that it was a destined love, decreed for her by the hand of fate that was taking good care of her. Eventualities were not important. What did matter was that fate had tested her with all manner of vicissitude and had found her never failing to give of herself.

Two beings then could testify to the goings-on in the Hostelry: the stork and Abu Musa, but neither of them had anything to say. Furthermore, they might well be the only two who had any inkling about the future, and yet they both seemed reconciled and content enough. Shamah thought that she would at least try to approach Abu Musa and ask if he knew what fate had in store for her. She had no doubts about the rumors that were flying around about his pilgrimage journey or about his being a holy man possessed of esoteric knowledge. He was simply a man who had finished up here and now was waiting patiently. There was nothing to roil his pure heart or cloud his visionary powers, powers that afforded insight into the truth. Were she to approach him, he would not be able to turn her away; as Pedro had said earlier, everyone was bound to like her.

Shamah knocked on Abu Musa's door, something she had never seen anyone do before. He opened the aperture, looked out, and waited to hear what it was she wanted. All she could manage to get out was a single request which she had not even thought of beforehand: "Sir," she asked, "would you allow my husband to spend some time with you during the day?"

"Yes," Abu Musa replied quickly and eloquently, "he can do so whenever he wishes." This positive response amazed Shamah; it was almost as though she had imagined him to be dumb.

After expressing her thanks Shamah hurried back to her own room. `Ali was not there, so she threw herself down on the bed and hid her head, just as though she had come home from an encounter with an angel in heaven. She was thrilled to have arranged this boon for her husband, since she was afraid that at this particular point in time loneliness and lack of work would make him miserable.

CHAPTER SIXTEEN

The first morning `Ali went out with Abu Musa, he followed him at a discreet distance so that the guards at the gate would not think them in any way connected. Just as he was trying to leave through the North-West gate of the city, the Sabtah gate, the guards realized who he was and stopped him. They asked him to wait for a moment before he could leave the city. The head-guard came out with a young assistant charged to do whatever he was asked. "I have no intention," said the head-guard, "of keeping you in the dark about the orders we've received concerning you. Every time you wish to leave the city through one of the gates, the guards at all the other gates have to be informed in case they allow your wife to leave. If she leaves the city, then you may not do so."

This ban on movement came as a shock to `Ali. He felt he should retrace his steps and inform Shamah about this new situation, something that neither of them had even thought conceivable. However he managed to quell his anger and simply waited around till the young boy came back, at which point they let him out.

He had no idea where to go, but then, looking towards the sea, he spotted Abu Musa waiting for him under a tree. He caught up with him, and the two men walked in silence till they reached the spot beside the sea where Abu Musa's cave was. Abu Musa went in and invited `Ali to follow him. The cave was at the bottom of a high cliff and open to the sea; it was large enough for a whole group of people. On the walls hung ropes holding clusters of fruits, dried vegetables, strips of meat, salted fish, clean cloths, and a bag containing paper and a wooden board with writing on it that the passage of time had almost worn away. In one corner of the cave floor there was also a jar of water and some pomegranate seeds.

Abu Musa prayed two rak`ahs, then left the cave carrying a basket. Heading towards a promontory that was being battered by the waves, he started gathering bits of seaweed and putting them in the basket. This went on for a while. He seemed to be making his selection with considerable care, either that or else the process involved some worship ritual that demanded an unhurried tranquility of mind. Abu Musa stood up, pondered, then bent down again, plunged his razor between the rocks, and withdrew it again—all this without the slightest sense of boredom. All the while, `Ali kept watching him, sometimes staring off into the distant horizon. He had the feeling of ridding his soul of all the filth of the Hostelry and expunging the din that assaulted his ears while there. Now he had forgotten everyone, save, of course, for the woman who lived by his side, organized his life, and nursed his soul's hurts. Shamah, the woman who knew full well that, when he went out with Abu Musa, he would be raising his sights above the sordid ground where their life together was being ruined; she it was who had sent him to the sea, with the idea of placing him in front of a mirror of her own self, she being like the very sea whose waves strike the shore and return to their place of origin. It was as if she wanted to see him move to some more expansive space, to place him in a blue firmament that would match the color of her own eyes. She was constantly worried in case he started feeling fenced in, something that would make him prey to the atmosphere of intrigue within which other people were making every effort to ensnare them.

When `Ali returned home, he told Shamah everything that had happened during his time with Abu Musa. He also told her that the two of them, Shamah and he, were virtual prisoners inside the city; for some pretext or other they were not allowed to leave. For an hour or so Shamah paid no attention to this further example of harassment from the rulers of Salé. What she wanted to hear about was details of his time outside the city and the activities of his companion. Shamah loved and revered the sea; she felt she could talk and listen to it. At the same time she was well aware of the way it had demolished the Sultan's fleet, sucking men into its depths, bringing death to great men, widowing wives, and orphaning children. Anything to do with the purity of the sea was a reflection of its Creator, in all His beauty and majesty.

From time to time Abu Musa would go back to the cave to eat, drink, pray, or, with motionless lips, read the text of a copy of the Quran that he took out of the bag. In all these activities `Ali would follow his lead, accompanying him when he went in or out of the cave, eating, drinking, and praying. Late in the afternoon they would return to the city.

Several days went by without them exchanging more than a few words. By now `Ali knew all his companion's rituals, which hardly changed from one day to the next. `Ali spent most of his time staring out to sea from inside the cave; it was as if the sea had come to occupy a special place in his inner being, working like some antidote to revive and open his heart. Now he knew that Abu Musa, his companion, spent the nights of ebb-tide by the sea—`Ali did not stay with him for those, and the nights of full tide in the Hostelry—when `Ali would be with him.

CHAPTER SEVENTEEN

One cloudy day Abu Musa and `Ali returned at their normal time to find the Northern city gates closed. The same situation applied to the other three gates too. Without saying a single word Abu Musa gave a broad grin, then turned round and headed back to the cave by the sea. As though responding to a signal `Ali followed him. It was dark when they got there, the twilight having vanished beneath the distant horizon. As they entered the cave again, their eyes grew used to the darkness. The sea surface reflected a dim light on to the promontory where the cave was, and that enabled them both to grope their way to a spot where they could sit.

Abu Musa took a flint out of the bag, struck it, and lit an oil lamp. He then performed the sunset prayer, albeit late, with `Ali beside him. Once finished, he reached for the pomegranates and gave `Ali a section, then took down some segments of salted fish and gave most of it to `Ali too. All the while `Ali kept watching this remarkable man. In this nocturnal setting he seemed even more mysterious and inscrutable than ever.

His brilliant teeth did not seem to fit either someone his age or someone who lived the way he did. Once he had finished eating, he rinsed his mouth outside the cave and cleaned his teeth with a toothpick he took out of a pocket. Reaching with his hand he delved into the bag hanging on the wall and took out a copy of the Quran. He started looking at it, and, as he did so, his features kept changing. It was as though the various expressions he adopted were a kind of encapsulated portrait of the meanings contained in the passage he was reading: thus he seemed to plunge in the deepest gloom, then quiet down and relax, and then almost gyrate in an excess of joy and rapture. Once finished with the Quran, he lay down, apparently almost unaware that anyone was there with him. He kept moving his facial features as though talking to himself in some way. Indeed one got the impression that he was actually following something that loomed in front of him. Then all of a sudden something gave him a jolt. He fell silent, frowned, and started rubbing his beard furiously with both hands, then his stomach, his back, his entire body; he looked as though he were itching all over, like someone plagued by lice or bedbugs. He kept this up for some time without seeming to get tired, and yet he did not seem to be in any pain.

All this affected `Ali profoundly. He had not the slightest doubt that it was all just one particular feature of the mysterious secrets linked to this man. It was therefore something he could never broach with him, neither posing questions nor offering assistance. As he sat there watching Abu Musa, his thoughts were distracted by concerns about Shamah: how was she faring, how would she understand what had happened, and how could she spend the night unharmed when he was not at home? He consoled himself with the thought that she was much too astute and mature to be scared. She knew whom he had left the city with, and Abu Musa, his companion, had not returned home either. She would be reassured that, in the company of such a blessed man, nothing untoward would happen. She would probably assume that after the evening prayer the two men had fallen asleep, and the sea had prevented them leaving the cave unless they were prepared to swim. `Ali had already described the location to her, so she could imagine it for herself. These and other explanations gave him some comfort as he gradually dozed off to the sound of the waves on the shore. Falling into a fitful sleep, he started snoring. Every time he woke up during the night, he remembered where he was and again rehearsed all the factors that reassured him about Shamah's safety. With that settled, he would go to sleep again.

At dawn Abu Musa woke him up to perform the prayer. `Ali took a close look at him but could detect no sign of sleep, exertion, or tiredness. He recalled that, before they had both

169

fallen asleep, Abu Musa had been rubbing himself all over, but now he was not rubbing himself or doing anything to attract attention.

They both washed, performed the prayer, and then headed back to the city. When they got there, the North gate was already open, as was the gate to the Hostelry. They both went in and knocked on `Ali's door. They found Shamah sitting there, as though she had not slept all night. She rushed over to `Ali, hugged him, and buried her head in his chest as though she really was on the point of bursting into tears but had managed to control herself. `Ali was surprised at how upset she seemed. He could smell perfume and assumed that it was for his sake that she had made herself up the night before. She had waited and waited for his return, something that she had never had to experience before. What also surprised him was that she did not ask what had kept him away. Instead he was the one who started explaining things to her and apologizing. He told her every detail about their night in the cave, about what Abu Musa had done—the prayers, the bag, the fish, the pomegranates, and the way he had gone into a trance during which he seemed to be conversing with hidden spirits. He talked about the sound of the sea and the light it gives off at night. Finally he told her about the way his host had spent the entire night scratching himself.

At that Shamah gave a start and pulled back from him. "What was that?" she asked. "Did you just say he spent the whole night scratching himself? How could that be? Did you ask him why he was doing it? Tell me everything that happened when he was scratching. When did he start? When did he finish?"

`Ali could understand Shamah's concern for the holy man. Her persistent questions made it clear that she was anxious to know what had been wrong with him and to look for a suitable antidote. That's the way she was, he told himself, always suffering on behalf of other people, sympathizing with them, and trying to help them as best she could. She was convinced that Abu Musa's illness had nothing to do with the dirt on his body or his outer garments which were actually extremely clean. If only he wore expensive clothes, he would be very handsome. Scratching parts of the body that itched was a well known malady, and the ointments to treat it were equally well known. Shamah knew all about ointments and the secrets of herbs. She could certainly talk to Abu Musa, suggest a cure, and thus strengthen her own ties to him; and, if that happened, she might be able to get him to open his heart to her. That was her ongoing quest. Indeed more than once she had wanted to wash his cloak and invite him to her home, so convinced was she of his blessed qualities.

So `Ali told her again how Abu Musa had scratched himself, what he had been doing before he suddenly started behaving that way, and how he had seemed to be performing some particular task without showing any sign of physical pain.

"That's enough," Shamah said when he had told her everything. "You've told me everything I need to know. Now I know what his illness is, but it's something we can't discuss with him. While ensconced in his retreat you have now learned one of his deepest secrets. He should not find out that you have told me about it."

`Ali realized that, when it came to proper behavior, he knew nothing compared with his shrewd wife. He was sure she was right. She got up and started making breakfast. She asked him to go to the market by the wall to look for some mulukhiyyah in which she could cook some lamb for lunch. He watched as she went over to take a nap in the hope of recovering some of her peace of mind. In fact, Shamah did not go to sleep. She wanted `Ali out of the way so she could do her utmost to keep her real emotions a secret. That was not only because of what she had just heard from `Ali but also what had actually happened to her during the night when `Ali had not come home.

CHAPTER EIGHTEEN

In fact the things that had happened to Shamah and her husband were directly linked to the itching fit that Abu Musa had had in the cave. That night someone had knocked on the door of Shamah's room. She assumed it was `Ali; he coming home late, she thought, because he had gone to listen to the sermon in the mosque after returning from the cave by the sea. She was astonished to discover her disgusting female neighbor, named for her slimy qualities, standing there with a smile on her face. "Two strangers are here," she said. "They want to speak to you." With that Tudeh stepped aside, and one of the two men came over and greeted her.

"Your husband's been invited to the Governor's house this evening," he said. "We've come to escort you there. Take a few moments to prepare yourself. If we take too long, the Governor will be angry."

Shamah was thunderstruck. She did not believe a word of it, but realized nevertheless that behind the invitation there

lay a threat. The command was deadly serious. There was
no room for refusal or procrastination; in situations like this
such strategies would be useless. She applied a little make-up
and put on an elegant dress covered by a grey burnous cut
from Amalfi cloth. Going downstairs, she found the two men
chatting with the doorman who appeared to know them both
well. One of them walked in front of her, the other behind.
They did not take her to the main entrance to the Governor's
mansion, but instead entered a small house in a narrow alley
with only one door; it backed on to the Governor's mansion
and seemed to be connected to it via a small door. Finding
herself in a quiet spot with no sign of people around, Shamah
fully anticipated some kind of disaster, but had no idea how
bad it might be or what precisely would happen. She was
invited to enter a splendid domed room of the kind she had
grown accustomed to in Ibn al-Hafid's house. Lit by two
lamps, it was filled with antique rugs and couches covered
with ornate silk draperies. In the middle was a brass table
with a bowl of fruit on it. Opposite the door was an alcove
large enough for a resplendent bed covered with a pyramid-
shaped awning.

It was not long before someone entered in whose presence
she had stood before: Governor Jarmun in person, the man
who had forced her to take off her veil when, along with her
husband `Ali, she had been brought in irons to the Governor's

residence. He greeted her as he entered, and she responded. With that he sat down, looking quite ill at ease. "There's no need to worry," he said. "I merely wish to use the opportunity afforded by your husband's absence outside the city to ask you about certain matters pertaining to the Sultan. I've been wanting to ask you about them for some time." With that, he started asking her questions about Al-Jawra'i and their marriage, about the reprimands he had received because of the marriage, and about the treasures that Ibn al-Hafid had stored somewhere inside his house, either in the cisterns or the walls. Then he asked her about the female servant who had accompanied her on the fateful expedition to the Eastern Territories. Had Shamah been told anything about the reason this servant had been sent to accompany her? Was she aware of the fact that Pedro, her husband's friend and a merchant who had only recently quit the Hostelry in Salé, had been spying on behalf of one of the Christian Princes of Al-Andalus?

Jarmun kept plying Shamah with these detailed questions and others like them. Shamah had only a little information to give him. Actually she started to feel less anxious now that she realized that the gates of the city had been shut specifically to keep her husband away and to give Jarmun this opportunity to question her. His motivations were entirely personal, namely the hatred that he continued to feel towards

Ibn al-Hafid, his voracious appetite for money, and the interests of the spy network operating between him and the police force in Fez that had kept its eye on her ever since she had married Al-Jawra'i (not to mention certain unanticipated outcomes, such as the requirements of Princess Umm al-Hurr's will that Shamah be released from the palace and sent back to Salé).

At this point, Jarmun changed the subject. "None of these issues matter to me as much as my wish that you work with me and not reject my friendship. I will know precisely how to help you avoid all the trials and difficulties now besetting you. I am even willing to overlook your husband's foibles, since I am totally convinced that he can bring the bustle of activity back to the Oil Hostelry and restore the former level of tax revenue, that being a matter that has made the city of Salé a subject of close attention at the Sultan's court in Fez. And, before we change the subject again, I'm going to leave you for a while so that you can try some of your favorite dishes which you'll find on that table on the other side of the room. And you can take a bath too, if you need to do so."

With that Jarmun left. Shamah responded to his suggestions and made a pretense of eating some of the food so as not to annoy the Governor. She was well aware that he might use the flimsiest excuse to humiliate her in whatever way he saw fit just in order to satisfy his own whims.

A short while later Jarmun came back. "You're still wearing the clothes you came in," he said without pausing for breath. "It's as though you're rejecting the honor we've bestowed on you by inviting you to visit us in our private residence and by involving you in our discussion about matters of importance both to the court in Fez and to you personally as well. Long ago you learned the correct way to conduct yourself and the protocols appropriate to exalted circles such as these. I don't think you've forgotten the kind of obedience that's expected from servants such as yourself."

Shamah lowered her gaze and said nothing. She could think of nothing to ameliorate the situation, and felt so humiliated that her brain refused to function. Certain things were just about possible, even tossing her off a cliff like some stone, but producing a response at this moment was not one of them, except as a groan perhaps. In such a situation comprehension, conversation, or discrimination, all such skills were out of the question.

Jarmun noticed she did not reply and moved closer. She sprang back. "I think you will come to appreciate," he said, "the difference between behaving properly with me of your own accord and having me compel you to do so." Shamah still stayed where she was without saying a word, and Jarmun did likewise. All of a sudden he felt an overwhelming need to scratch his beard hard, then under his armpits, and then between his toes. He kept staring at the rug on the floor, the couch coverings, and the walls, as though looking for the insects that were causing him such agony but finding nothing.

Shamah kept snatching glances in his direction, her eyes lowered. She was scared that he might suddenly decide to assault her when she was least expecting it. She watched in astonishment as he kept scratching himself all over as hard as he could, and then she noticed that he needed to scratch a spot on his back that he could not reach. He left the room. Hearing the leaf of another door being opened, she could envisage Jarmun using it to scratch his back.

After a while he came back into the room and sat down again. Once again he had a fit of scratching all over his body and had to leave again. She got the impression that he had taken a bath, stayed there a while, and then come back. Barely had he sat down before the itching started again. This routine went on for a while, with him coming in, then leaving again, but without ever ridding himself of the itching sensation. Eventually he became infuriated. "Did you bring some magic potions with you or something?" he asked. "This time, you've been unlucky. Next time it'll be worse!"

He left the room, passed through the passageway from one house to the bigger one, and did not return. After a while one of the guards who had brought her there came in and greeted her as though she had completely satisfied his master. "Let's go back," he said. She went out into the alley, just as scared as when they had arrived. By now it was midnight; the only people on the streets were guards at crossroads and nightwatchmen at the stores in the markets. The doorman of the Hostelry was by the gate when they arrived. As he saw the two guards and Shamah approaching, he opened the gate. Shamah entered, and the two guards went on their way. By the time Shamah reached the fourth floor, she had no doubt in her mind that the noise her feet had made had woken up two women at least who would be eagerly waiting to see what time she had returned: Tudah being one, and Pedro's daughter the other.

Shamah did not sleep a wink. What disturbed her the most was that of all people Tudah had been the one to knock on her door and tell her that the two guards had come looking for her. That confirmed for sure that she was working for the Governor and was fully implicated in a conspiracy against her. In fact, ever since Tudah had come to live in the Hostelry, Shamah had had her suspicions. From that moment on she had loathed Tudah, but now she had confirmation of the truth of the situation. Worst of all was that this evil woman would now be able to exploit last night's episode in order to force Shamah to do her will. The implicit threat would be that Tudah would tell Shamah's husband precisely what she imagined had happened while Shamah was a "guest" at the Governor's house.

Shamah went through agonies as she tried to work out the best solution. Should she be totally frank and tell her husband about the Governor's "invitation" and what had transpired at his house? Or should she keep it all to herself, for fear that he would not believe what had actually happened? With this second scenario an additional worry was that `Ali might fall prey to doubts and delusions about his wife, and they would be difficult to dispel. All that might cast a pall over their married life, something that had so far remained strong in spite of all the trials and tribulations they had both endured.

Shamah decided not to tell her husband what had happened. However, no sooner had `Ali told her about Abu Musa's antics in the cave—how at a particular point during the night he had started furiously scratching himself, than she bitterly regretted not telling him everything as soon as he came home. If she had told her story first, he would have realized at once that the Governor's itching fit was entirely due to the actions of Abu Musa. The holy man had brought his genuinely spiritual influence to bear on the situation. Had she done that, her husband would never have doubted her version of what happened in the Governor's house. But now the opportunity had passed. Even at this stage she might have considered telling her husband what had happened. If he seemed to disbelieve her, she could rely on Abu Musa to confirm her innocence. All this was, needless to say, based on the assumption that Abu Musa was indeed the one whose actions had rescued Shamah from a really dire situation at the hands of the Governor. Had she refused to submit to his will, he would not have hesitated to have her killed. However Abu Musa steadfastly refused to get involved. The reason may have been that he himself did not fully understand every-thing that had happened. It was either that, or else his fit of scratching had actually been unconscious. The forces of good had taken control and made use of powers hidden deep inside him—without him knowing anything of their existence or the reason why he was invoking them. In any case, whatever may have been the reason, Shamah now bitterly regretted her mistake in not telling her husband what had happened. In reasoning the way she had, she had had the very best of intentions, but now she was victim to a sensation she had always managed to overcome, namely fear. Had she decided to ignore the possible consequences and tell the truth, she would still have been protected by the forces that had always managed to intervene during previous trials; and those forces much preferred honesty to other considerations. Good intentions were of no use if they were based on assessment of impact. Initiatives had to be founded on principles with their own precedents; and she had broken one of them today, namely honesty. So now she was suffering because she had surrendered to a fear, one that would inevitably lead to others like it. Furthermore, she had chosen a compromise that satisfied the parameters of neither the seen nor the unseen worlds in proving its veracity or conformity with fate. Worst of all was that Shamah's two women neighbors could now exploit to the full the fact that she had left the Hostelry without her husband and gone to the Governor's residence at night, only returning home much later.

Next day the town-crier whose job was to announce the Governor's edicts in a loud voice came to the Oil Hostelry. He told the merchants that, from now on, anyone who received merchandise and failed to sell it within one week, or who did not pay the required tax on such merchandise even if he had not sold it yet, would have to pay the special tax called the stock-storage tax, based on a percentage that would be charged every night according to the value of the merchandise in question. In fact, the reason why the Governor had decided to impose this tax was that there had been a relative decline in tax-revenue from the Hostelry and the city as a whole. He had received a letter of censure on the matter from the chief tax-collector in Fez, along with a warning as to the consequences. The Governor had immediately consulted his aides and coterie about the most effective ways of raising tax-revenue. The suggestion had been made to launch an attack on speculation, whereby merchants would deliberately wait for prices to go up and keep goods off the market until demand increased and they could get the price they wanted.

As news of these measures spread, merchants in the Hostelry and others from outside the city were infuriated. Just a few days later word spread that three major merchants had left Salé for Sabtah, leaving their stalls in the Hostelry with no agent—a sure sign that they had left for good. However, the Governor did not take this news as any kind of warning sign. To the contrary, he instructed his tax-collectors to assess the value of goods currently in merchants' hands so they could pay the necessary storage-tax; they were to make full use of his guards for support as required. It so happened that at this very time most of the Maghrib region was hit by ten full days of torrential rain; which meant both that no new merchandise arrived and also that no customers came to transport the goods from Salé to other regions. As the month came to an end, the tax-collectors started computing the amount of tax owed by merchants, and several of them were unable to pay. Many of them took refuge in mausoleums, seeking sanctuary and a means of escape from their obligation.

CHAPTER NINETEEN

At sunset on the day following this tax-inspection procedure, Shamah's husband, `Ali, was returning to the Hostelry
after his afternoon session with Abu Musa when he encountered two of the Governor's guards who followed him up
to his room. They informed him that he was summoned to
appear before the Judge next morning. He was required
to certify to the doorman that he had indeed received this
summons.

When he told Shamah what had happened, neither of
them wasted any time trying to guess what the charge might
be this time around. After all, it was the Governor making
the accusation. For that very reason it could involve anything
imaginable and even other things that occurred neither to
them nor other people. As Shamah bore in mind her own
recent experience with the Governor--something that she
had kept secret from her husband, she was well aware that
this new development could well be much more serious than
anything they had had to face thus far. With that in mind,

she convinced `Ali that, when he left the Hostelry in the morning, it was better for her to leave as well, taking her most precious possessions with her—her gold jewelry and precious jewels, gifts from Al-Jawra'i and Umm al-Hurr, that she had brought back from Fez. She would take refuge in the home of the Sharifs* of the Banu Sa`d household who claimed Qurayshi lineage and now lived in Salé, having fled from Al-Andalus when their leader was killed at the battle of Al-`Uqab (1212 AD). The rulers of the era had accorded them a status of high respect, one that exempted them from certain liabilities and protected them against the rapacious instincts of Governors and the like. Shamah was intimately acquainted with the family members and knew every female personally; in particular she had a favored position with the wife of the Marshal of Sharifs.

So `Ali appeared before the Judge, with the Police Chief also present. The Judge ordered `Ali's hands tied and then required the clerk to read from a document which contained the charges against the accused:

—activities with sorcerers and magicians involving the concoction of amulets injurious to certain of the Sultan's retainers;

Sharif: a direct descendant of the family of the Prophet Muhammad, someone possessed of particular sanctity and respect within the Muslim community.

--incitement of merchants to abandon Salé and quit their stalls, leading to a shortfall in tax revenue;

--discovery of a wine-skin in the accused's former store-house, duly searched by market-detectives, who testified that the wine in question had been at the facility till just a few months ago;

--failure to observe the purity required of a Muslim and the invalidity of his marriage to Shamah.

Once the charge-sheet had been read out, the Judge ordered `Ali committed to his prison, a single room no larger or less filthy than the Governor's jail-cell. `Ali would stay there until another court-date when he would answer the charges laid against him.

Never before had the people of Salé heard of such a complex indictment or such a variegated set of charges. The news rapidly spread all over the city. That very afternoon, the Marshal of the Sharifs, Abu `Abdallah al-Sa`di (in whose home Shamah had now taken refuge) went to the Governor's residence. He was admitted and welcomed by the Governor. "You noble Sharifs are always welcome," he told Abu `Abdallah, "and your intercessions are always granted, except, that is, when the matter involves people who defame the sanctity of Our Lord, the Sultan. After all, his sanctity is also yours."

The Marshal understood full well the import of the Governor's words. He was also aware that the Governor's spies had told him about Shamah's move to his, the Marshal's, own house. Once the Marshal had taken his seat, the two men resumed their conversation, mostly about the future of commerce in the city and the shortfall in tax revenues. The Marshal tried to find out some details about the charges against `Ali, but the Governor pretended to be completely unconcerned about the entire matter and changed the subject. Instead he discussed the invitation the Marshal had received from the Sultan's court in Fez to attend the sessions of the conference that the Prince of Believers was holding during Ramadan.

When the Marshal left the Governor's residence, he was very worried about Shamah's now imprisoned husband, the foreigner who had recently converted to Islam and was now facing an uncertain fate at the hands of a Governor who was hell-bent on using all sorts of retainers and schemers for his own sinister purposes. When the Marshal reached his home, he immediately sent someone to bring the Judge there after dinner without anyone noticing.

When the Judge, named Abu Jabr al-Madhun, arrived, the Marshal greeted him warmly. He outlined for him the benefits and support that would be his if he were prepared to reveal to the Marshal details of the charges leveled against `Ali Sancho.

"The evidence I've relied on," the Judge replied, "is contained in the Police Chief's report. The accused can only avoid the consequences of these charges if you intercede in person with the Sultan in Fez."

"So what is the nature of this magic of which he stands accused?" the Marshal asked. "Who among the Sultan's retainers is the alleged victim? Which accomplice is alleged to have worked magic upon the accused's demand?"

"The Police Chief has stated," the Judge replied, "that judgment must be made as though the evidence were clearly established. If the Judge insists, the person injured by the crime may reveal his identity to the Judge alone. Such secrecy is necessary because state interests and personal reputations are at stake."

"And what will be the sentence for this crime, should you impose it as you seem to imply you will?"

"Whipping and imprisonment," the Judge replied.

"And what about inciting merchants to leave and the negative effect on treasury revenues?"

"His Amalfi agent has left the city," the Judge replied. "He was someone whose initiatives greatly benefited commerce in Salé. Then the accused accepted the position as his agent when he was not qualified; he submitted false reports about his profits; he encouraged Pedro himself to leave, the accused being someone whom Pedro himself had designated an agent. Lastly three other merchants have left too, all of them affected by the accused's losses and by the bad reputation he gave the Oil Hostelry."

"And what sentence do you propose for this charge, should it be confirmed?"

"A fine equivalent to his entire property."

"But he doesn't own anything," the Marshal pointed out.

"What I mean is that the fine will be equivalent to the losses in tax-revenue for the past months. It's an enormous amount. He will have to pay it or else suffer further whipping and elongation of his jail-term. His wife undoubtedly has enough wealth to reduce the enormous amount somewhat. He'll be doing himself a big favor if he doesn't claim not to own such an amount, but instead offers to pay at least a half or a third."

"What evidence do you have of his drinking wine or not being a good Muslim?"

"That he drinks wine is proved by the discovery of the wine-skin in his storehouse. We handed it over to the market-inspector. Some of his experts have managed to confirm that it's of Malaga manufacture. It has been used to hold wine for so long that it's impregnated with it; that evidence comes from people expert in smell and using a special technique by exposing it to fire."

"What about evidence of his not being a good Muslim?"

"He has not purified himself completely by being circumcised."

"How can you claim that his marriage to Shamah is not completely valid?"

"According to police reports, one night, with a big grin on his face, he addressed a question to the preacher in the Grand Mosque: what was the legal status of someone who had married a Muslim woman thinking she was a widow and had paid the bride-price accordingly, only to discover on their wedding night that she was actually a virgin. The only way such a question makes any sense is if he's the person involved."

"So," the Marshal asked, "what do you see as the sentence for these three charges?"

"The legal sanction for drinking wine, compulsory divorce from his wife, and a requirement that he pay the Christian tax if he persists in living in Muslim territory."

The Marshal sat there, listening in amazement as the Judge saw fit to condemn the accused man on such flimsy evidence.

"Fear God, man!" the Marshal warned him. "There is one Judge in heaven for two down here..."

"Esteemed Marshal," the Judge responded, "there was a time, I realize, when people's hearts were filled with piety, which made it much easier for our predecessors as Judges to enter paradise. But in this era of ours, God's servants have started behaving in a much more brazen manner, and that makes our task that much more difficult and risky. Any Judge who aspires to paradise after death seems on the point of hurling the people of this world into a hell of intrigue kindled by evil forces on a daily basis. The Governors of Our Lord the Sultan are working to stamp it out; it is we servants of the Sultan who purchase the paradise of security for all people. Everyone working for the cause has the right to exercise independent judgment, albeit based on dubious grounds. The protection of people's lives and values falls squarely on the shoulders of people like us. But, no matter how much support is provided, it will never be enough to cater to all people's rights or to compensate for all the trouble involved in keeping a vigilant eye on their comfort and security while they sleep. How then do you expect me to deal with charges against this Christian plasterer who claims to have become a Muslim and to have been adopted by my pre-decessor, when His Excellency the Governor is determined to make him an example to all those who would make fun of him; especially when he has failed to attract commerce to the city? How much respect can he command when, after a period of commercial expansion enjoyed by us all, something from which the tax-authorities in the capital benefited, we now look on as the whole thing is about to disappear, leaving us all in a state of misery and deprivation? Why did citizens

of Salé welcome a recently arrived foreigner so lavishly, when
he declared himself a Muslim without offering any evidence
to support his claim? If he had really converted, then
Muslims would have been justified in their praise. If he'd
crossed the river and fought in Our Lord's armies, wouldn't
he have earned some of the booty to which he would have
been entitled? How can we possibly just let him lead a life
beside the sea without having any idea of what plans he is
hatching up? Maybe he's expecting some enemy to arrive
by sea, so he'll be the very first person to raise his standards
and prepare his forward troops. The man has meddled in our
lives and our business, and the citizenry—God forgive them
all!—has committed a grave error by allowing him to marry
a Muslim virgin on the grounds that she was a widow. The
truth of the matter is that Al-Jawra'i was not man enough
to consummate the marriage; he merely put her in his bed as
a kind of sport when he proved incapable of fulfilling one
of the obligations of married life. Just think: this servant-
woman was accorded the honor of living in the harem of one
of the Sultan's most trusted retainers where she learned all
about the routines of our leaders and the organization of the
government. Can't you see how in moments of weakness
she might reveal state secrets to her husband, the kind of information that could be used against us if foreign merchants
who come to our shores were to reveal them to our enemies,
particularly in those regions that, as you well know, harbor

inimical intentions towards our rulers? Let's suppose for a minute that the rumor being spread around the city is true: that His Excellency the Governor is harassing `Ali because he wants this servant-woman who is currently `Ali's wife for himself. After all, isn't the Governor, himself someone of noble birth who acts on our behalf in keeping us all safe and secure, more worthy of possessing such a woman should he wish to have his way with her? Can't you see that it is no credit to either religion or chivalry for people to remain so blind, indeed so stubborn, when it comes to acknowledging the infinite virtue of the Governor who is responsible for safeguarding their homes and streets and protecting their property and family honor? Such an acknowledgment of blessings is only right and proper. Anything else is to be condemned."

As the Sharif listened to this stupid Judge's list of pretexts, he could only feel the deepest disgust. Nor did it escape his notice that he was also included in the list of people who were supposed to submit to the rulers' will because they were the ones who allegedly protected people from fear. The implication was that there was nothing wrong in being afraid of rulers and in acknowledging that they deserved every conceivable kind of concession in accordance with their expressed desires, even if something genuinely sacred were involved.

"Who precisely are our rulers protecting us against?" the Sharif asked.

"From hidden enemies who are poised to strike," Judge Madhun replied. "Not only that, but they also protect us from ourselves. Every single community among us is at war with itself, every person is in fact two people with a long-established feud going on inside. Those who wish to break out of such chains and refuse to obey have to transform themselves from a single entity split in two internal parts; in other words, to launch a war to the finish against himself. Once we have all achieved that sense of inner tranquility, we will be able to relax and the three Judges whom you have mentioned will all enter paradise."

"Now I realize," retorted the Sharif, "that I have nothing to say either to you or to your master, the Governor. 'Only steel can blunt steel.' "

With that the Judge departed, feeling as though he had been summarily dismissed. The Sharif returned to his quarters and sent a servant to fetch the legal scribe who always helped him compose official documents relating to the Sharifs. He dictated the following letter:

After "In the name of God…," to our august Lord, the cham-
berlain of the Sultan's court, we would beg to bring to the attention
of his exalted Majesty the fact that the Governor of Salé is harass-
ing the womanly integrity of the servant of the late (by grace of
God) Lady Umm al-Hurr, widow of his Majesty's revered father.
The matter concerns the widow of the illustrious Judge-martyr,
Al-Jawra'i---may God bestow His mercy on him! She is, by virtue
of the will of the Lady Umm al-Hurr, which Our Lord has vouch-
safed through his munificence, entitled to all due favors. However,
the Governor of Salé has imprisoned her husband (who is a convert
to Islam) and is now intriguing to have her divorced so that he can
satisfy his own lewd desires. This is our information. Farewell!

The Marshal of Sharifs in the Salé region.

He then dictated another letter to Governor Jarmun himself:

To the Governor of Salé as appointed by the Royal Court in Fez:
After the required greetings to Our Lord, we wish to inform you that
the woman named Shamah, daughter of Al-`Ajjal who resides in
the Oil Hostelry, has sought shelter in the House of the Sharifs. She
has requested protection among our children as a means of escaping
from the sense of panic that has overwhelmed her because of the
way you have arrested her husband and placed him in the Judge's
custody. We have acceded to her request in light of the testaments
of our Lord in Fez, his father, and his father's father—may God

Almighty show them all his bounty—dealing with our total discre-
tion in such matters and in regard to all those who seek refuge with us.
The woman in question possesses a will from the exalted lady, the
late Princess Umm al-Hurr, widow of our Lord's own father,
signed by His Majesty in person and ordered executed by seal of
His Majesty's own chamberlain and noble assistant who is still in
office. With that in mind, we have yesterday dispatched an urgent
letter to the capital city demanding confirmation of the privileges
previously decreed for this woman and those whose well-being is
linked to hers, by which we mean her husband who is currently
being detained in your prison. It is our conviction that he has done
nothing that either diminishes his own faith or honor or his belief
in the sovereignty of our Lord, the Sultan. We hereby instruct you
to await the response from the capital city. No Judge, tax-official,
or agent may execute any judgment against the prisoner in question
until such time as the opinion of the Sultan's officials is known.

That will resolve the matter satisfactorily, and only on that basis
will the matter be resolved.

The Marshal of Sharifs in the Salé region.

When Jarmun read this letter, he was furious. Having
succeeded in putting both `Ali and Shamah in prison at the
same time, he hated the idea that the Sharif could interfere
with his plans. What surprised him most was that never

before had the Sharif involved himself in a matter to the extent of sending a letter to the capital city. He was equally surprised to learn from the letter that Shamah possessed a document that spelled out in detail her rights as granted in Umm al-Hurr's will. He had assumed it was just some purely temporary memo to Ibn al-Hafid. A challenge of this kind was not something he had taken into consideration. He was well aware that the Sultan's current policy involved currying favor with the Sharifs. That removed any hope he may have had of nullifying this Sharif's intervention in this matter or of finding some way of preventing the dispatch of a response from the Sultan himself.

What made Jarmun even angrier with the Sharif was that every day the latter sent one of his servants with Al-Khawdah to visit Shamah and offer her comfort in her time of trial. Both of them would then bring food and other essentials—clothing and the like—to the prisoner, all of which arrived in good order and without hindrance thanks to the royal prerogative that the Sharif enjoyed. Jarmun became yet more concerned when certain senior officials in the capital to whom he would regularly send bribes let him know that the Sharif's letter had indeed been received. Now it would be impossible to prevent the Sultan from hearing its contents. The Governor was strongly advised not to insist on prosecuting `Ali, since that could well lead to the issuance of a royal command to conduct an inquiry into the important matter of which he had accused `Ali, namely inciting merchants to leave Salé. There was an implicit risk involved, namely that the person charged with conducting such an inquiry might well turn out to be an official who did not think highly of Jarmun; indeed they might well dislike him to the point of enmity.

CHAPTER TWENTY

After receiving such a letter from Fez Jarmun realized
that the key problem, one that might well end his career, was
the shortfall in commercial tax-revenue. He was convinced
that something could be done to recuperate the losses and
sought advice from some of his counselors. They advised
him to anticipate the usual deadline by demanding that rental
agreements for the stores, warehouses and stalls in the Oil
Hostelry be renewed early. They also suggested getting
phony bidders to force up the cost of rental fees. However,
the plan backfired. In fact, the very opposite of what was
intended occurred: as soon as the bidding started, the
majority of merchants chose to vacate their premises, and the
phony bidders were exposed. When the first stall was put up
for bids, neither the tax-collector, market-inspector, nor the
Governor's own deputies who had come to attend the bidding
process, were shrewd enough to realize what was happening.
They did not even catch on as they watched several merchants
vacating their premises. They carried on with the bidding till
the very end. Apart from Abu Musa's residence which was an

endowed property for jesters and clowns, `Ali and Shamah's, whose owners were abroad, and those of Tudah and Julia, Pedro's daughter, which were not put up for bidding, only five agents acting on behalf of owners with capital in distant cities accepted the increased rents. They went along with the bidding, albeit conservatively. Even then, they forced the market-inspector to cancel their bid if, upon contacting their owners, they discovered that he refused to accept the new costs. When Jarmun learned what had happened with the auction, he was livid. He swore at the supervisers of the operation and promised them a cruel revenge. He then sent word to the Senior Merchant, requesting that he make every effort to persuade merchants quitting their stalls and shops not to do so; for the time being there would be a purely formal agreement to pay the additional amount demanded, but it would be annulled within two months at the most. In reply the merchants said they did not want any contracts written. Indeed they demanded the immediate abolition of the storage tax that had recently been imposed on them, since it was destroying their business and making it impossible to speculate and wait for the right moment to display their goods at an appropriate price.

The merchants' attitude infuriated Jarmun. He had no desire to make it look as though he was giving up on a decision he had made. As far as he was concerned, any kind of climb-down would diminish his prestige, that being the mainstay on which his authority was founded. For him that consideration was much more important than people's lives and welfare. Just to show how annoyed he was with anyone prepared to stand up to him, he sent some of his guards to force the merchants to vacate their premises and to remove their goods in a single day.

CHAPTER TWENTY-ONE

Having initially sought shelter in the Marshal's house, Shamah now took up residence there. At this point she had come to realize that her husband's prison-term would not be short unless she could do something to protect him. As long as Jarmun had her husband locked up, he would not show her any respect. Above all, she was eager to know what were the charges against her husband so that she could counteract his fiendish schemes.

In the Sharif's household Shamah found herself the center of a good deal of solicitous attention, since news of her move to his house had spread throughout the city. The ladies of Salé made a point of coming to see her, albeit under cover most of the time, in order to offer her comfort and consolation and any kind of help she needed.

Shamah may have been of lowly birth and may have been forced to reside in the Oil Hostelry where merchants and tradesmen of all regions resided. However, as far that the Sharif's family was concerned, she deserved enormous respect, not only because of her familiarity with the corridors of power and nobility, but also because she had chosen her lot with a convert to Islam, a skilled craftsman whose decorations of buildings were widely admired for their exquisite taste and creative instinct.

But Shamah was not satisfied simply to bask in all the affection and admiration that embraced her as a refugee in need of love and pity. She started involving herself in household affairs, and especially the kind of refinements at which she was particularly adept. She would share her opinions about various matters, and sophisticated society ladies would inevitably be impressed. The topic might involve dinner preparations, banquets, choosing furnishings and crockery, or teaching such skills as embroidery, sewing, necklace-stringing, choosing jewelry, designing new patterns for the jeweler or fresh segments of cloth for the milliner, distilling exotic kinds of perfume from flowers, roses and plants, producing smelling-salts from fruits and tree-roots, or making different types of make-up from tree-bark, plant extracts, powders, and creams. As if all that were not enough, Shamah was also the fount of all knowledge for the household women when it came to the best strategies for consorting with husbands or treating particular feminine illnesses to which they might be exposed, and the most subtle and delicate ways of evoking hidden sentiments. And all this does not even mention her knowledge of religious devotions, recommended actions, and pious intercessions appropriate to every conceivable situation.

Even had Shamah not possessed all the above-mentioned virtues, she would still have been endowed with a bounty of heaven-sent gifts, all of which radiated through her femininity. Such was her beauty that one was reminded of God Almighty, so much so that to regard it as something sinful, something even to lead one into temptation, was an impossibility. Instead she herself regarded her very beauty as a heavy burden that she had to bear. Even the most jealous of women used to discuss her beauty with their menfolk, like something surpassing that of all other women. For her part, Shamah was eager not to attract the slightest attention to herself in case it led to trouble of some kind. That is why she always seemed so concerned to distract people's attention from her appearance, something that was forever changing, just like the sun itself. In her case it became something cool and tranquil, so as not to burn everyone close to it. She kept herself out of the public eye through personal modesty, self-denial, and always helping other people. She regarded her beauty as a blessing and a curse. Even so, she was concerned that, by trying to keep it hidden, she might seem to be ungrateful or to be trying to snuff out God's gleaming light when He might wish to have it exposed to the light of day. In spite of it all, she made a point of accommodating her beauty through the sheer grace of her movements, her gentle smile, exquisitely mannered conversation, sweetness of temperament, modesty, and continual activity. There was all this, and so much more, which combined to make of her beauty an inspiration that extended its wings over all creation without arousing the slightest degree of jealousy. Shamah was like a peacock, a bird that certainly arouses admiration but that simultaneously puts the observer in mind of both beauty and serenity.

CHAPTER TWENTY-TWO

The Oil Hostelry's bankruptcy hit Salé like an earth-
quake. Everyone in the city assumed the bankruptcy would
have a impact on the city's tax payments to the capital city
and especially on their own lives. As commerce in the Oil
Hostelry dried up, many people lost their livelihoods: merchants, agents, registrars, contractors, artisans, store- and
stall-owners. The collapse also affected mule- and donkey-
porters, porters who used their own backs, swindlers and
con-men, masseurs in public baths, bread-sellers, makers of
baskets, palm-leaf containers and bags, meat-sellers, and
itinerant women who sold henna and kohl; even people who
read at festivals and banquets and others who earned a living
from coins deposited in collection boxes. Everyone felt the
dire effects of the economic collapse. It felt as though their
luck had run out and the world had decided to turn its back
on them. For some reason or other, they all deserved to be
flayed by such a harsh punishment. Ever since Jarmun had
been appointed Governor of the city, they had all labored
under the heavy hand of his arbitrary behavior, and yet they

had still managed to earn a decent living from the flourishing trade at the Oil Hostelry. Commerce had been transported to it from a wide variety of countries and then distributed, so it had come to serve as the living pulse of the entire city.

The caravan of pilgrims returning from Mecca was accorded the usual elaborate welcome upon its arrival. That particular year they invited the pilgrims from Tamisa to spend the night in Salé. A visit to the public baths and the barber could serve to rid their tired bodies of the encrusted dirt of the long journey. In addition, the wealthier among them could purchase whatever they needed from the city's markets. However, the Salé pilgrims were shocked by the level of despondency that seemed to have descended on the city, almost as if the entire community had suffered some kind of hemorrhage that had drained all its strength. It did not take them long to discover the true extent of the disaster that had struck this once flourishing city, a port that had been successful for many centuries. But now the time had finally come when it had been deserted by all the merchants and financiers from many countries who had used it as their base of operations. Among the returning pilgrims were merchants who had owned stalls and stores in the Hostelry, but who were now desperate as they saw themselves facing unemployment and an uncertain future.

This year too the pilgrims from Salé included some people who once again claimed to have seen the man known as Abu Musa who lived in the Oil Hostelry during the pilgrimage rituals in Mecca: they had spotted him during the standing period in `Arafah, walking between Al-Safa and Al-Marwah, and performing the circumambulation of the Ka`bah. Following their return to Salé, they all announced this information at their gatherings and supported each other's versions of the events. None of them said that Abu Musa had come up to him, spoken to him, or answered any questions. All they said was that they had spotted him. They had no idea how he had managed to slip away, thus avoiding the need to reveal his real identity so that there could be no room for denial or doubt.

This year people making such declarations were not bothered about the possible consequences of the Governor's determination the previous year to probe the veracity of these reports—including investigation and cross-examination. This time the claims failed to produce any reaction from either the Governor or the Chief of Police. It may have been because the logic of last year's inquiries demanded that such rumors needed to gain a certain currency before people would be completely convinced of the possibility that men of virtue could exist in virtuous times. It was either that, or else the authorities in Salé had used all their tyrannical instincts in imposing new tax measures and were now in an even deeper mess than ever. The whole question was preoccupying their attention to such an extent that matters of lesser importance did not bother them.

When people heard stories like these, they again started looking more closely at Abu Musa in Salé. Everyone concerned with the issue added to the collection of tales by recalling different aspects of this remarkable man's life that showed the extent of his piety, things that had previously not attracted the slightest attention. Some people with commercial links to the East reported that a Byzantine ship-captain had described a man from Salé to him. The description matched Abu Musa exactly. This man, the captain reported, had asked for passage from Alexandria to the Maghrib aboard his ship, but he had refused the request. During the voyage to the Maghrib, every time the ship docked in a harbor, this same man had showed up at the port, laughed in his face, and then vanished. This had gone on for so long that the ship-captain had almost lost his mind. Even so, till now no one had dared approach Abu Musa or share in his activities, apart from exchanging pleasantries and attending Friday prayers. The only exception was the newly converted Muslim, `Ali Sancho, who followed behind when he walked to his cave by the sea, but without ever talking to him. No one knew how all this had come to pass. In particular, no one was aware that the reason why Abu Musa had agreed to this procedure was because he had been asked by a woman. To this day she herself could not explain how she had gone to see him and how, when he had looked out at her through the aperture in his door, she had said something that till that very moment had not even crossed her mind. His quarters in the cave by the sea were no secret to anyone. There was no door, and inquisitive shepherds used to go into it quite regularly. They never touched anything, the dried fruit that he gathered from a patch of land that no one owned, and the dried salted fish that he caught from the sea and cured in salt that he bought once a year for the price of a single day's work as a porter in the Hostelry. He took whatever oil he needed for lamps both here and at his residence in Salé from the oil jar in the hermits' sanctuary. Most of the time he ate just seaweed.

By now Abu Musa had become a major topic of conversation in Salé salons. The stories that were told reminded them of people from the past, ascetics, miracle-workers, and holy men. The topic was even discussed by religious scholars at their regular meeting. "Never before," said their chief, "have people been prepared to acknowledge the kinds of qualities that they're now attributing to Abu Musa. In my opinion, that is because he neither owns nor wants anything. As a result, he has no need of rulers." One of the other attendees objected. "Godliness," he said, "involves helping other people, not being satisfied with your own status." With that, the arguments started and various evidential texts were cited. However, it all led to an acknowledgment of the fact that people can be subdivided into three groups: those who harm no one, but only help them; those who neither harm nor help people; and those who harm people without helping them. The people listening to this discussion and the various hints and allusions that were part of it were well aware that the primary topic of debate was actually Jarmun, the Governor of Salé. While acknowledging the harm he had done, they asked themselves whether he had actually provided people with any benefits. On the other hand, had his rival, Abu Musa, benefited people in any way, it being readily acknowledged that he had not harmed them? People supporting the Governor's cause said that he had in fact brought benefits by stamping out burglary and street-crime. Those attendees who supported Abu Musa's beneficial effects protested that God never hurts people, holy men among them; the benefits that they bring are, more often than not, invisible. To support that view they cited stories of miracles performed in days gone by. There was, for example, the story of the lunatic whose place in the Oil Hostelry Abu Musa had taken over. People had come out of the mosque and found him playing with a female donkey; he claimed to be repairing damaged planks on a ship. Some people laughed at him, others even tried to chase him away. But later on, sailors from Salé who had been on the ships in the Sultan's fleet during the disastrous expedition to the Eastern territories and had managed to make their way to land some days later reported that their ship had been holed and they had indeed watched a man who looked exactly like this lunatic repair the damage—it had been a genuine miracle. The meeting ended on a sarcastic note punctuated by bitter, morose comments. "Wouldn't it be wonderful," one of them said, "if Abu Musa could restore commercial prosperity to the Oil Hostelry or else make good use of his hallowed status to rid us of the miserable tyranny that is strangling us to death!"

Had Shamah been attending this session or heard the conversation among the shaykhs, she could have provided ample evidence to show, without any possibility of argument, that Abu Musa's beneficence was an undeniable reality. She was still deeply affected by what had happened when the Governor's aides had brought her to their master's house. His violent scratching fit had prevented him from carrying out his vile intentions. She also remembered what her husband had told her, how he had spent the night with Abu Musa in his cave where he too had been scratching himself.

However that was not a story Shamah could tell anyone, even if she had been in attendance at the shaykhs' session. The nightmare still affected her, and it was not about to go away. Another woman, in fact two other women, knew enough about the circumstances to raise doubts about it, even though neither of them knew what had actually happened. Beyond that, the story had two separate parts to it: one was the part that she clearly knew, namely what had happened to the Governor in her presence; the second was what her husband had told her, namely what had happened to Abu Musa as he watched. The linkage of the two accounts was certain enough as far as she was concerned, and only someone with very particular motivations would be able to cast doubt on it. But any attempt to use it as a means of proving her own innocence, should occasion demand such a course of action, would require that the entire affair be presented to a fair Judge. Two witnesses would be required, who could both confirm what had actually occurred, namely Governor Jarmun and Abu Musa; and that was, needless to say, out of the question. Thus, in the absence of such a process of human judgment, Shamah remained innocent in the eyes of God alone. Where people were involved, Shamah was well aware that, even if at some point in time she were declared innocent, they would still remember that there had once been an occasion on which she had been accused of misconduct. Accusations of such a kind are halfway to proving that the crime was actually committed.

CHAPTER TWENTY-THREE

Following Governor Jarmun's decision to imprison `Ali in the Judge's residence two full months went by. `Ali was not brought to trial. Everyone in Salé waited for the response from the court in Fez to the request of the Marshal of the Sharifs. The time the decision was taking was roughly what the Sharif himself expected, but Shamah began to get really worried. She suspected that Jarmun had either found a way of ensuring the Sultan did not see the letter or else had bribed someone in the capital city to arrange matters so that the plight of this defenseless prisoner should be ignored and the influence of Jarmun himself, with all his sterling efforts at protecting tax revenues, should be enhanced. Then she imagined that the letter had actually arrived and the Sultan had issued an order providing restitution for the wronged man, but the entire matter was in limbo. No one was following up on it because everyone was preoccupied with other matters, or else Jarmun had used his usual corrupt methods to achieve his own ends.

However only a few days after Shamah's anxieties had started to intensify, the reply to the Marshal's letter did indeed arrive. It contained a command from the Sultan that `Ali, the husband of Shamah, should be released immediately, that Shamah herself should be given a testament of regard renewing the commitments made in the will of Princess Umm al-Hurr, and that her family should be included in such regard and protection. Neither she nor any of those who belonged within her family circle were to be subjected to any form of harm or interference on the part of any governmental authority, nor could she or any of her relatives be charged as the rest of the populace were, even in matters involving obligations and duties owed to the Sultan.

Jarmun ordered `Ali released immediately and gave him back some of the money he had confiscated. He apologized to `Ali for the unfair treatment he had received, due, he said, to false information passed on to him by the police in Salé. At the same time Jarmun sent the Marshal of Sharifs a copy of the document from the court in Fez regarding Shamah, and notified the Judge and all senior officials in Salé of its contents.

The Sharif put on a party to celebrate the success of his efforts, since God had granted him such a boon in removing a terrible wrong, something demanded by his exalted position and by the expectation that he would always be ready to defend what was sacred and to protect people's honor and virtue.

Jarmun did not seem the slightest put out by what had happened, nor did he show any compunction in carrying out the Sultan's orders. It was as if in both situations he would be quite willing to carry out his master's instructions and exert every effort to please him. In fact, Jarmun regarded his own gross behavior and transgressions as being part of his efforts on the Sultan's behalf; even his personal wishes and desires could be subsumed within the same category. For the people of Salé, the way in which the prisoner was released and the Governor's ongoing assault on the virtue of a woman who was whispered to be the victim of a whole series of intrigues and maneuvers had finally been brought to an end, this was nothing less than a huge slap in the face for Jarmun. Furthermore, it had come from the Sultan in person, not to mention that it served as a clear warning to the Governor, something he should bear in mind in future. The entire episode made people feel as though a huge weight had been taken off their collective chest. It was a virtual victory for their crushed sense of self-respect.

Throughout the city the echo of freedom resound-ed. It had come from the court in Fez to Shamah, and had resulted in the release of her husband, `Ali, whom everyone had presumed to be innocent but no one had dared to help either by word or deed. In fact, Shamah felt an enormous sense of frustration, in that a tyrant had been on the point of exercising his own will against an innocent man with nothing and nobody there to stop him. Many was the time she asked herself about this disastrous set of circumstances. Were chivalrous qualities, she wondered, simply a pleasant myth, whose existence and continuity involved not being subjected to this type of test; was courage restricted only to war situations involving two foes? What made her feel even more cheated was that she would really have preferred the victory of right over wrong to have come about as the result of a decision made by a particular group or even an individual rather than by this Marshal of Sharifs, so that the Muslim community as a whole would earn the esteem of her husband who was newly converted to the faith. It was almost as though she was afraid he might recant, or that these hard-ships might lessen his fragile belief. Indeed she may well have thought (and even wished) that what bound the two of them to each other was in fact two pledges: one pledge to his God in the Islamic faith, a powerful pledge since no trial would lessen it however tough it might be; and a second pledge to her, one that could not conceal the nature of harsh reality. His adherence to the first of the two, she thought, should be the stronger. These notions convinced her that the most important thing was for him to remain her husband. She could heal his wounds, and he would come to realize the wisdom of the old saying that "whatever happens will happen."

CHAPTER TWENTY-FOUR

People in Salé assumed that Shamah and `Ali would not
return to their room in the Hostelry, especially since they had
both received an explicit honor from the Sultan in person.
Not only that, but the Hostelry was now a different place;
with the merchants' departure, it was basically devoid of any
honorable type of activity. Governor Jarmun had started
lowering the rents for empty rooms, shops, and storehous-
es, and kept giving leases to a series of utterly inappropriate women who had moved there from other old hostelries
or from houses in the district under the North Wall of the
city. For all the same reasons the Marshal of the Sharifs
also assumed that Shamah would take his advice and change
her place of residence, most especially because he wanted
her to retain her connection with his household. His own
family members were especially anxious about it because
Shamah had managed to charm the entire household with
her company, her affectionate demeanor, and her consummate skill in all the feminine arts. It was certainly possible to
find an appropriate residence for them both even beyond the

bounds of the endowment properties over the rent of which the Governor had control.

However, with a typical display of modesty Shamah insisted on returning with her husband to live in the Hostelry. The truth of the matter, something she kept even from her own husband, was that she believed in Abu Musa's piety. Of all people he was the one whom she most preferred as a neighbor. She alone knew that, whether consciously or not, he had been deeply involved in the peculiar events that had accompanied her summons for a nocturnal visit to the Governor's residence in Salé. Shamah was also completely convinced that all the rumors about his participating in the pilgrimage each year by way of instantaneous transfer were true. She recalled the way he had immediately agreed to her husband's accompanying him to his cave by the sea most days that he went there and was well aware of the serenity that this arrangement afforded her husband, and remembered fondly the sympathy Abu Musa had shown both of them on the day when the Governor had vented his anger against them and everyone else had taken to their heels. She was not willing to entrust her husband's welfare to anyone, keeping in mind the fact that he was far from his own family and his conversion to Islam was fairly recent.

He could be even more affected by contact with people whose

faith was not particularly strong and with others who were not very rigorous in their adherence to the proper practice of their beliefs. There were times when Shamah actually thought that it might be better to abandon this whole idea; her husband might be better served if he had the chance to mix with believers of all kinds and confront whatever the world might throw at him. Then his resolve would be strengthened and his faith would take root, just as long as he continued his practice every evening of sharing with her all the things, both good and bad, that had happened to him or that he had seen and heard that day. All that was needed was to correct a few particulars. Even so, Shamah could not rid herself of a fear that had recently started to nag at her, as though she might lose her husband and be deprived of his company.

The Marshal asked Shamah and her husband to stay in his house till they were both fully recovered from their ordeal. After several weeks many people congratulated them on the conclusion of a nightmare that had caused them both many sleepless nights—the way the Governor had chosen to harass them both, and particularly the way he had put `Ali in prison. Now the two of them went back to the Hostelry and could see for themselves the extent of the changes that had happened in the building which had gained its reputation for commerce and whose occupants had previously been merchants. Now all but a few of them had left. The only people left on its four floors were Abu Musa and eight women: Tudah, Julia, Pedro's daughter, and six new female occupants who had taken up residence while Shamah and her husband had been away.

After a few days Shamah had learned to recognize the faces of her new neighbors, although she made no attempt to get to know them well or to suspend the necessary level of formality between them. Even if Shamah had wanted to know the details of each woman's life, her sensitivity and goodness of heart were such that her only motivation in inquiring would have been sympathy and affection.

CHAPTER TWENTY-FIVE

BIYYAH:

A diminutive red-head who from an early age had grown up in the household of one of the Zanati shaykhs near Anfa, the ancient city of Tamisna. She was a servant-girl in a large house with dozens of people in it: the shaykh, his brothers, other female family members and servants, wives, mothers, sons, daughters and daughters-in-law. These people were well settled and had a long-standing tradition of farming and horsemanship. The yardstick for beauty was good health, pure blood, and upright posture; a particular feature was how tall they were. When other women who were jealous of Biyyah wanted to insult her, they would point to her shortness and say she came from the mountains. She may have been a little plump, but the service she offered left nothing to be desired, so much so that wives and mothers of children used to fight with each other to get Biyyah to help them; she could save them a lot of trouble when every twelve days it was the turn of one woman in the household to prepare the food and drink for the entire household, to change the seat-covers, and so on.

As she grew up, Biyyah added to her talents a skill in dancing to the tunes of the Zanati chants that were used to fire up horsemen and soldiers, but there was something else as well that aroused feelings of pride and amazement, as well as envy and hatred: the long, cascading length of hair which women likened to a horse's tail. She used to gather it up in a big bun on her shoulders, and would not let it down in case it dragged along the floor. Neither salt air nor sea moisture had any effect on it, unlike other women whose hair would turn curly and look unattractive. Whenever her rivals in the Zanati shaykh's household grew particularly jealous of the way her hair looked, they would say the reason was that she hailed from the Masmudah mountain people who would regularly drink aquavit made from grapes, something they had learned from the Jews with whom they lived. Biyyah would become alarmed whenever she heard this kind of talk. "I don't even know about aquavit," she used to say, "and I've never drunk any. My mother may have done so, or maybe she rubbed my hair with it when I was young. God has given me what He has given me." Pondering the situation, she was perplexed at the way people insisted on attributing anything beautiful to sinful origins or faulty intentions.

When the women who envied Biyyah could find no way of hurting her or suppressing their aggravation, they started saying that she was so busy fussing with her hair that she neglected her duties or that she wasted time in perfumiers' shops buying combs, henna, and cloves. Her response would be to state that the way she took care of her hair was an expression of gratitude for such a boon. Even so she found herself subjected on more than one occasion to actual harm as a result of this very same boon. For example, she fell sound asleep one night after spending a great deal of effort helping with entertainment for visiting tribes; next morning when she woke up, she discovered that fully two-thirds of her hair had been cut off using the cropping-shears used on sheep. She could not believe it, and assumed that she was still having a horrible nightmare, but, once she had rubbed her eyes and confirmed that it was true, she panicked, then raised a hue and cry, swore, and started crying. Before her eyes she could see the culprits who had dared to do such a dastardly thing. When people in the household woke up, some of them tried to comfort her while others enjoyed her distress. Everyone realized that the person whose idea it had been was not the person who had done the dirty deed; there was no way of telling who the instigator had been, while the actual perpetrator could be neither accused nor even identified even though his identity was known. Indeed it was not merely known, but fully acknowledged: one of the shaykh's own teenage sons, a spoiled brat and the child of his favorite wife.

The history of Biyyah's dealings with all these many children is, as is the case with many servant-women of her type, a very long one. She used to give rides to the young ones and exchange pleasantries with the elder ones. In fact, it was they that caused Biyyah's departure from the Zanati shaykh's household. Two young men got into an argument over the way the coverings should be arranged, and both of them insisted that Biyyah be the one to do it; neither of them would allow Biyyah to perform the service for the other.

The shaykh had in fact already decided to dispense with Biyyah's services but without sending her back to her parents in the Tadlah Mountains; he realized that her future did not lie there. He made a deal with one of his brothers who was to leave on a Zanati caravan to an annual festival at the mausoleum of a Rikraki martyr who had been buried on the left bank of the River Bu-Rikrak. Biyyah was one of the women who was ordered by the shaykh to accompany his brother on the caravan. On the third day of the celebrations one of the Zanati caravan's leaders suggested to Biyyah that she go with him for an hour in order to hear a troupe which was renowned for its spiritual dance and its panegyrics. Biyyah, who by nature was susceptible to all kinds of music and song, only needed to hear the voices of the troupe's chanters before she became one of the very first women who were so affected by the music that they sprang into the middle of the circle and started dancing in time with the melodies and tambourine-beats—all in a state of extreme ecstasy. Biyyah's hairband fell off, and her hair cascaded to the ground. She danced to left and right to the pulse of the voices, and her breasts swayed with her. Everyone was fascinated by what they were watching. All the spiritual notions implicit in the tunes and panegyrics vanished as they stared, mouths agape, at the glistening bouquet of hair on this petite woman who was now so entranced that her wrap had fallen off to reveal her festive dress.

Among those watching the spectacle was a middle-aged woman from Salé. She continued to watch Biyyah and started planning a future for her; as though her experience in the ways of the world had allowed her to read the life of this woman or else she had heard her anguished cries and her yearnings for a better life that till now had been shrouded by deprivation. Immediately after Biyyah had emerged from her trance and settled down again, the woman from Salé rushed over to Biyyah, wiped her forehead, picked up her wrap, wrapped up her hair, and helped her leave the ceremony. As soon as she could, the woman started asking Biyyah questions and soon learned everything about her. The sun was about to set. Suddenly Biyyah sprang up and started looking for the man who had brought her to the ceremony. He had vanished. The woman from Salé stayed with her as Biyyah rushed back to the place where her Zanati family had been camped. How great was her surprise when she discovered that the people who had brought her there had packed their bags and left before the time they had agreed upon, namely dawn the next morning.

Biyyah wandered all over the place, then sat down and started crying because she realized that she had been brought there just so she could be thrown out with the trash, exactly as they do with a rabid dog so that it won't find its way back. Now she understood everything as she thought back and went over all the details to confirm that the Zanati shaykh's household had indeed tired of her. But she had been too naïve to realize that this trip to the festival had actually been a trick to get rid of her. She had never wronged anyone or behaved badly, but it was in the interest of the house that she had served since her childhood to dispose of her without mercy or sympathy. Those arrogant studs, she realized, believed in family solidarity above all else; that was their pretext for all kinds of behavior. Ever since she had become aware of her own developing femininity, she had thought that the idea of building a family nest such as any woman dreamed of would involve being married off by the shaykh to one of his subordinates. She and her husband would then remain in the household's service, as had happened with so many servant-girls before. But, as the days had gone by, she had got the impression that this dream was starting to disappear; the reason being all the rumors that enveloped her and all the unfair accusations of stirring up rivalries among the shaykh's own sons and his nephews. It became clear to Biyyah that this type of slander was enough to see her removed from her native soil, even if she occasionally imagined that some man might come along and ask for her hand, ignoring her petite stature that was such a stigma amongst these people whose men and women were so notably tall.

Biyyah now realized that she could not go back to the Zanati household; she had been abandoned, and no excuses would be accepted. Now here was this woman from Salé who had already realized what she was thinking and offered answers to her despairing questions. Biyyah assumed that the woman would play the role of someone who had been assigned the task of receiving her from the people who had brought her there and steering her towards a new life.

Biyyah had no choice but to accompany her into Salé. The woman lived in a house by herself, with only an olive-skinned maidservant. From the very first day Biyyah realized that her hostess had started treating her as a mistress does a servant. Even so, she also showed a certain degree of kindness, which led her to think that the woman felt a particular concern for her. Men of very neat appearance used to visit the house, and the woman was always anxious to make sure that Biyyah served the guests on such occasions.

The woman forced Biyyah to perform particular services in people's houses, but she had no idea how much her mistress charged for them. She found herself like an indentured slave, a prisoner of this woman who obviously had broad connections with men of wealth and influence in the city.

Biyyah soon became aware of the kind of life she had been forced into and abandoned all hope of ever enjoying a normal sort of life. She learned all the routines connected with the life of a woman in her position. It took many years, a whole series of arguments, and the intervention on her behalf of certain influential personages with whom she too was now well acquainted, for her to achieve even the minor feat of being rid of the woman who "owned" her,. Thus it was that, on the recommendation of some of the Governor's aides, Biyyah was one of the women ordered transferred from a street where people had grown tired of her to the Oil Hostelry now that the merchants had left.

CHAPTER TWENTY-SIX

`IJJAH

A name meaning "perfume." As a child she was sold in a desert market during a drought season. It was her mother's husband who sold her in a market at the foot of the mountains; the price was a few bags of barley. She was bought by a Bedouin from the plains who used her as a shepherdess for his animals. However when she grew older, her master's wife became jealous of her, so he sold her to a group of dancers who used to tour around the homes of notables in cities and tribal encampments.

She was the youngest among five colleague women who used to play for joyous occasions involving both men and women. There were four men in the troupe; the leader was a sixty-year old composer of zajals who was very well known. He treated the members of his troupe with great kindness, performed in public with great dignity and respect, and subjected his accompanists to very rigorous training. This was all part of a pact with his own teacher in this particular art, someone who had practiced it with a special veneration; clearly, if the art was indeed practiced with the permission of its exponents, then it had to be done in accordance with the demands of traditional chivalry. He taught each member of his troupe, and especially the women, how to develop their art to the point where the audience was delighted and even transported by the performance, going so far as to arouse anyone to displays of immodest behavior.

'Ijjah learned how to play the flute, to tap the tambourine, and to use hand-bells to accentuate rhythm and sound out tunes. She remembered a number of songs, and over a period of time became the troupe's star performer, with no rival; it was as though her energy was being constantly renewed and her fame was spreading far and wide. She never dared ask any of her companions in the troupe how she had come to join them, but she was convinced that they all had stories much like her own. The details did not matter as long as she was willing to be treated like the servant of this man whom the women in the troupe regarded with a mixture of fear and awe.

At the end of spring once the wedding and party seasons were over, the troupe's leader took his group to visit the shrine of a holy man in the mountains. With them they took enough food to last them for several days of comfortable lodging. In a market at the foot of the mountains they purchased fine clothes for the men and women; they were all delighted at the way in which the troupe's leader was showing his satisfaction at the way they had all worked throughout the summer and traveled hither and yon to respond to invitations from party-givers. In the end they had managed to collect a sizeable sum of money from the tour, and the reception that they had received wherever they went suggested strongly that, as time went by, their popularity would only increase.

When the troupe reached the famous mausoleum, they visited the site, and their leader gave charitable donations to the holy man's descendants, to the indigent, and to Quran readers who resided there. They then went to a rented lodging house, and the leader asked for crepes with lamb's meat. The women set about the task with joyous hearts and prepared a wonderful meal. Once it was over, they all gathered round to perform for themselves. It was a fabulous evening, and as song followed song, the chief prayed to God for himself and his fellow-artists, with acts of devotion and humility, to which they all chanted "Amen."

When the session was over, the leader addressed them all. "Boys and girls," he said, "'Ijjah cannot remain unmarried at her age. If she agrees, I'll marry her tomorrow according to God and His Prophet's ordinances and under the beneficent eye of his holy man at whose shrine we're staying. You are all my witnesses and know that I purchased her myself. Tomorrow I have things to do in a nearby village. I'll go there at dawn. Take enough money to buy a sheep from a shepherd, slaughter it to celebrate this ceremony, give some of it away as alms, and prepare a feast worthy of the occasion—God willing!"

The men congratulated their leader and wished him a long life of happiness, then he and the other men left to go to their own sleeping quarters. The women were left to themselves. `Ijjah was in a state of shock, having just heard something that had never even occurred to her. She had trained herself to put any idea of marriage right out of her head; she owned nothing and had no mother or father to concern themselves with her daily life. Her craft was one in which she herself was indispensable; she devoutly believed in the sharing of profits and the existence of a master who was even kinder to people than they were to themselves. Had she given any thought to the ways in which her current life might be transformed, it would have involved one of the hirers of the troupe or a spectator being taken with her and haggling with the leader to sell her to him for an irresistible amount. Even so, she realized that such a man would have to be an army officer, a navy captain, or a foreign merchant; no member of the nobility would agree to take as a wife a woman who had been working in a touring dance-troupe.

The five women all gathered around `Ijjah, trying to lessen the shock for her. They told her that they had all gone through the same routine: the leader of the troupe had bought them, trained them to work, and then at the appropriate age married them for a couple of years. After that he had divorced them and given them the choice of either staying with the troupe or going her own way, free and divorced. No man in the troupe was allowed to marry any of the women members. If he did or if a woman showed any interest in one of the men and marriage was contemplated, the leader got rid of him and brought someone else in to replace him.

The leader of the troupe married `Ijjah, but this time things were different. By now he had reached an age when he did not have the heart to treat `Ijjah the way he had done his previous wives. His love for `Ijjah only increased, and that drove a wedge into the midst of the group. Things reached the point when he would frequently absent himself from performances. His health started to deteriorate. One night, while they were performing in Salé, he fainted in the middle of the performance, and was confined to bed in a hostel for a long time. The members of the troupe hung around waiting for his health to improve, but, when their situation became precarious, he dismissed them all once and for all. The group broke up, and the members went their own ways. `Ijjah stayed beside her husband's bed, looking after him and performing in the homes of the local nobility in order to provide for him. Two months after the group had dispersed, he died. `Ijjah stayed in Salé and from time to time joined some musical troupe to perform at ceremonies for a wage. On such occasions she was exposed to all the indignities that women in her position have to suffer.

CHAPTER TWENTY-SEVEN

MALLALAH

Mallalah's father was a school-teacher who worked under contract for village communities; after a year or so he would move from one village to another. Mallalah's mother had died while she was still a baby, and her father had not taken another wife, anticipating that his daughter would soon be getting married herself and not wishing to upset her. He loved her to distraction, and found himself severely criticized for doing so in an environment which disapproved of coddling children in case it spoiled them for life. However he could be forgiven this trait since he worked in a profession which was far removed from the rougher aspects of bread-winning.

He taught his daughter how to read; he used to sit her down in the Quran school and have her hold the writing-tablet. When it came to memorization or paying close attention she was as much involved as the other pupils, and she managed to spend most of her childhood among boys. There was no aspect of their lives that could be kept hidden from her. In fact she used to argue with them and subject them to her demands, knowing full well the power that her father had over them. Many of the boys hated her for that very reason, although there were some who chose to take advantage of her affection for her father by bringing varieties of food for her to offer her father from the various households in the community.

When signs of maturity began to show in Mallalah, her father decided to ask some of the women who kept coming to request charms and talismans to cure illness and strengthen emotional resolve to take her under their wing and keep an eye on things.

However, Mallalah showed no signs of a desire to consort with other women. As time went on, her father became gradually more alarmed because he found himself unable to contemplate being parted from her if she were to get married, while her staying with him when she was of marriageable age would certainly harm his eligibility for serving as a traveling teacher in village Quran schools. He could not imagine her agreeing to stay with her maternal grandmother or one of her aunts. He was also distressed because she promised him to keep performing her prayers, but did not keep her promise.

At this point it was totally inappropriate for her to be sitting by his side while he was teaching. At the same time it was also extremely boring for her to spend the whole time on her own in the room where he was staying, most especially because there were times when he would have to be away at night because of wedding ceremonies, funerals, and other such occasions. She would not learn how to cook because the community would always make prepared food part of the teacher's contract; nor did she learn how to wash clothes, sew and perform other duties she might need in life because the children whom the teacher was instructing did all that as part of their duties.

One night the teacher returned home from a ceremony to find his daughter in tears. That made him sad and he insisted on asking her what the trouble was. She looked him straight in the eye and told him with an unusual frankness that she wanted him to marry her to so-and-so, who was one of his older students who had finished the syllabus and gone off to farm. He in turn asked about the precedents to this request. She replied that it was hers alone; he knew nothing about it. She went on to say that she would either get married or else throw herself down the mosque well from which people drew water for washing themselves.

The teacher realized that she was in deadly earnest and

broke down in tears himself. However he soon recovered and calmed her down. "I'll arrange everything tomorrow, God willing!" he said. With that she gave a big smile and fell sound asleep.

The teacher now sent word to his former student explaining the entire situation and requested that he keep the whole thing a secret if he was unwilling to accept the proposal; if he was willing, then he should ask his family to make the request.

The student was really in no position to refuse since his teacher was as good as being a father to him; to have refused would have been a matter of disobedience. In any case Mallalah was not a bad choice, provided that she could rid herself of her well-known impetuosity once she was married and had children. Beyond that the student's mother and brothers could not refuse a request of his since, as a memorizer of the Quran, he was their passport to the world to come. They all felt so proud of him every time he stood up before the entire community and took the Imam's place in reciting half of the Quran during the prayer on the Night of Power, all of it from memory and without a moment's anxiety.

So the student agreed and sent his relatives to ask for

the teacher's daughter's hand, not knowing that it was in fact the girl herself who had been the initiator. The community leaders undertook to provide the bride with her trousseau and to prepare for the ceremony on the seventh day of the Feast of Al-Adha. Mallalah moved to her husband's house and insisted that she not touch a saucepan or do any cooking. Her husband and his family all put up with her laziness out of respect for the teacher. In less than two months however, Mallalah left her house in the morning and went to see her father in the mosque. She asked him in tears to terminate her marriage. She said she wanted to be divorced and for her father to move from this village to another one sufficiently far away so that she would never again have to listen to a man whose company bored her to death and whose very smell she loathed. Neither her father, her husband, nor his family, nor intermediaries brought in by her father had any luck in persuading Mallalah to change her mind.

The student then agreed to his teacher's request that he divorce Mallalah, and the father agreed to his daughter's request that they move to another tribal region. They had hardly settled in to the village Quran school before Mallalah was doing the rounds of the homes and making a display of her impetuous behavior once again. The community was divided over this topic: some people wanted the teacher's contract to be cancelled since his daughter's behavior was not appropriate for the status that a teacher was supposed to have; others were of the opinion that the problem would be solved if one of the villagers asked for the daughter's hand in marriage.

However it was the daughter once again who chose the man she wanted to marry: this time it was a loafer who was the muezzin's son. The teacher had barely made the suggestion before the man accepted on condition that the teacher should pay for all the marriage expenses and their married life thereafter. This time the teacher could see no way of not accepting since the man in question was not one of his own students and his daughter was already under a cloud as a divorced woman.

It only took a few weeks before things soured between the wedded couple. The husband had no compunction about hitting his wife every time she showed some of her normal recalcitrance or refused to obey her husband's orders regarding those services that a wife is supposed to offer. Every time Mallalah's father saw the marks on his daughter's body where she had been hit, he burst into tears. In this case however, Mallalah was very fond of her husband even though she was not prepared to submit to his authority.

The teacher could not stand to see his daughter suffering in this way, while the villagers were dissatisfied about his staying in the community when his status was being so clearly compromised. So the teacher decided to move on, but his daughter refused to allow him to leave without taking her with him. Divorce therefore inevitably followed.

The teacher now took his daughter back to his own folk, hoping to find some respite from all his troubles before he would have to look for another tribal location in which to practice his profession. Meanwhile Mallalah found the supervision to which she was subjected by her relatives intolerable; she defied them wherever possible and exposed the entire family to scandal. Once the teacher's money had been spent, he went to the Northern tribes to look for work, in the process ignoring Mallalah's pleas and threats that he should not go or that he should take her with him.

A few days later a merchant caravan arrived in the village, heading from Al-Hawz to Salé. Mallalah struck a secret deal with one of the men to hide her in his merchandise, and he took her to Salé. A few days later he moved on and left her there. At this point the city showed her its teeth, and she found herself forced to surrender to a labyrinth of compulsion and lack of choice. Given that she could no longer return, she even forgot where she had come from.

KABIRAH

A cobbler's daughter from Azmur, she was well proportioned and had pleasant features and a piercing gaze. As soon as she became self-aware during early adolescence she regarded herself as the Cleopatra of the age, deserving praise from all her mother's companions and destined to marry some prestigious person of authority or else an amir or one of his relatives.

Whenever she went to get water, she used to let her female companions leave and stay behind. She would wait for the water surface to settle down and then stare at her reflected image, totally entranced as she adopted various poses: content, then angry, smiling, then frowning; screwing her face up, then relaxing once again, as though she were anxious to prove that with her kind of beauty she could overcome any flaws. In fact she wished she could turn into two separate people, just so that one of them could enjoy the other, front and back, without a great deal of bother. She protected her face from the sun, her hair from the wind, her legs from water; never for a single day did she believe that her fingers needed any henna to enhance their beauty. She never stopped staring at her girl-friends so that she could compare herself with them: eye for eye, brow for brow, waist for waist, nose for nose. If she discovered another girl who was a perfect beauty, she would make a point of saying: "Yes, but my ear is so delicate and well-suited to mouth and face that no other girl can possibility match it." It was her opinion that if her own mother were to appear at some festival, everyone would know her and pay attention because she was so-and-so's daughter. As for her father, even though he spent his entire day punching holes in the shoes of shepherds and peasants and enduring the stench of leather, she felt he could lord it over other men and claim some kind of kudos because of his beautiful daughter. At all events, the greatest hope of Kabirah's parents was that one day through their daughter they would earn a position of prestige in society.

There came the day when the son of a cobbler colleague of Kabirah's father came to ask for her hand. She was furious and swore, assuming the whole thing was a plot against her; she refused to allow anyone to talk about it. Then the son of a local milliner's store came to ask for her hand, and she advised him to keep twining yarn for his father till he found a suitable girl. Now it was the turn of this young man's mother to beg that the entire affair be kept secret.

Next in line was a young man whose father was a snake-charmer who collected poisonous snakes and who claimed to be the devotee of a local saint who had given him enough confidence to serve as an antidote to snake-bites. By exhibiting snakes in market-places and treating people who had been bitten he managed to earn the kind of living which was totally unprecedented for someone in his profession or for anyone who did manual labor. This time, it was Kabirah's mother who undertook to deliver the response to the offer; it took the form of a gruff refusal, something that led to a nasty exchange of comments and insults between Kabirah's mother and the young man's. And that is how the story of Kabirah, the cobbler's daughter, developed: the arrogant girl who refused all offers of marriage, shamed both mothers and fathers, and went against all manner of custom and tradition—and all because she was so deluded and vain, the whole thing became the talk of the town of Azmur.

Years went by but no one forgot about the way Kabirah kept refusing all offers of marriage. No knight on a white horse appeared who might offer nature due praise for having created a girl such as the cobbler's daughter and consider her beauty reason enough to close his eyes to her humble origins and social status and her total ignorance of the proper way to behave as a bride in a noble house.

With every passing day Kabirah was staring spinsterhood in the face, so much so that the women of the quarter started calling her "Kabirah too old to get married." That made her parents very sad, she being their only child. Things got worse when Kabirah began to display symptoms of an illness that people described as the mark of the jinn.

"A Jinni sultan has loved her for her beauty since she was a girl," someone explained. "He's the one who has thwarted all offers of marriage. Now she's his bride, and from time to time he possesses her."

Kabirah's mother got a certain degree of consolation out of this interpretation of the situation, and even her father would mumble incoherently about it when asked. Even so, the idea of Kabirah being somehow betrothed to a jinni monarch did not excuse the father from the need to summon the most celebrated experts on spells and talismans in order to fight this possessing spirit and get rid of it. The process involved the father in a lot of expense, time, and effort. Nor was he spared the need to drag his daughter on visits to the tombs of various local saints and spending nights at their mausoleums. On days when Kabirah was recuperating from being possessed in this way she would treat everything as pouring salt on an aching wound: the slightest comment from her mother would turn into a criticism of her condition, as though she were somehow responsible for it; simply hearing the sound of a band or the joyous cries that accompanied engagements, weddings and other celebrations, or merely a snippet of news shared by a neighbor on the pretext of asking for some salt or yeast, all this would be enough to trigger memories of how she had attended an initiation rite at the home of her first would-be fiancé and a wedding feast put on for her second or third.

All this managed to make Kabirah detest her own self. She was almost ready to take revenge on it, so strong was the revulsion that welled up inside her. She began to be haunted by fantasies that made her lose her common sense and make light of the possible consequences of her actions. She made a decision to seek a solution to her personal problems somewhere other than this city that had mercilessly destroyed her fondest hopes and sent her dreams up in smoke. She had been wrongly punished, she felt, for feeling proud of something that not everyone had, namely beauty.

Every noon Kabirah used to look out from the balcony in her house which gave on to the lofty promontory overlooking the mouth of the River Azmur and mull over these ideas. She spent so much time up there that she had memorized the movements of all the vessels that came up the river to load or unload cargo, to bring in fish, or even to fish for shad in the river itself. She paid particularly close attention to the captains of the vessels that made their way in and out of the river and was able to recognize which of them was local and which came from abroad. From their flags she could tell which vessels came from other ports, and especially from Salé because there were so many of them. She concentrated on these Salé boats and settled in particular on a medium-sized vessel with the pronounced prow that was the prized feature of the boat-factory in Salé. Every time this particular boat came into the estuary, the captain would be standing in the bow—a very tall man with a strong, muscular body and tanned cheeks that reflected the sun's rays like mobile mirrors. He stood there, just like a mast that uses its weight and straightness to keep the boat on an even keel. There he stood, with bare shoulders and a blue headband on his forehead, just like a sailor in the midst of a sea battle. All he was wearing was a leather loin-cloth and a yellowing pair of trousers. In Kabirah's imagination he would be wearing leather shoes tied by a long cow-leather lace made specially for sailors.

For weeks on end Kabirah watched no one else and crafted in her own imagination an entire tale involving this man whom she did not even know. She thought of moving the tale ahead quickly in case he decided to change his weekly destination to some other port and disappeared. She had no doubt in her mind that, even amid all the flowers that adorned the balconies and thrived on the humidity and saltiness of the river air, he had inevitably taken notice of her. If he wanted, he could easily find out which particular street her house was on. Since he had obviously been coming to Azmur for a number of years he probably stayed overnight and could therefore identify the exact house.

One fine weekday at the usual time the prow of that special vessel appeared, pushing back the waves as it entered the estuary. Kabirah locked the balcony door behind her and took out a white handkerchief that she was planning to wave. She hid herself from the inquisitive gaze of her neighbors and made quite sure that the person in the boat was the man in question. Conquering her bashfulness she started waving the handkerchief. She saw that the sailor had noticed but did nothing to reply; she realized that many eyes were observing activity at the estuary mouth from the balconies, so he could not do anything by way of response to her waving; had he done so, he would have placed himself in a potentially difficult situation. Even so, she was sure that he had seen the woman waving the handkerchief and realized that she was the same one who was always sitting on the balcony but not making any gestures. He was eager for her to be aware that he had noticed her greetings, or, more accurately, her message. He kept looking in her direction till his boat disappeared round the bend where boats would tie up so as to stay out of the wind.

Just before sunrise next day, that being the day when the Salé vessel would leave, Kabirah was on the balcony again waving her handkerchief, and the boat captain was in his assigned spot at the bow of the vessel. This time however he continued to stare at the balcony until the boat had left the estuary and turned to the right in order to hug the coast and head north.

When the boat arrived the following week, the same procedure took place. Kabirah was certain that her message had arrived, and she kept waiting for an answer, worried all the while in case this little game went on for some time and her dearest plans for rescue were thwarted again. However, that very evening between the two evening prayers there was a knock on the door of Kabirah's house. Her father was still at the mosque. When Kabirah opened the door, she saw a woman standing there. She told Kabirah that a sailor with a message from a relative of theirs in Al-Andalus wished to inform her that he was staying in the Strangers' Hotel. If they wished to pick up the message, they should send someone to get it just before dawn on the following day when he would be leaving. Kabirah was about to say that they had no relatives in Al-Andalus, but she recovered herself and told the woman that someone would come and get the letter at the time suggested.

Just before dawn Kabirah disguised herself by wearing one of her father's woolen jallabahs* so as to fool the night-watchmen and port guards. Close by the Strangers' Hotel she ran into a Sudanese slave; the distinctive nosering he was wearing made it clear he was a sailor. When she went over to ask him where to go, it turned out that he was one of the captain's crew. Once he had found out that she had come for the message from Al-Andalus, he grabbed her hand, took her over to a corner where the street lights did not reach, and then unrolled a piece of linen sacking he had under his arm. He told her to get into it, then grabbed the sack and under cover of darkness ran with it towards the port. Kabirah heard him stop and talk to some people who may have been guards. Then he seemed to be walking on some planks and going down some stairs. Finally he put the sack down gently and let her out. She found herself in the cabin of the boat. There she sat, trembling with emotions that were a mixture of fear and anticipation of a happy outcome.

Kabirah stayed sitting where she was as the boat swayed from side to side; she could hear voices, but no one came to see her for several hours. Then the door was opened by a man with dark complexion who may have been the one who carried her onto the boat. He smiled, asked her how she

Jallabah: an ankle-length garment worn by men in the Arab world.

was, and put down some food and drink for her. With that he disappeared, closing the door behind him. A few hours later he came back, picked up the dishes, and indicated to her that she could go outside and find some water in case she wanted to wash before praying.

For a whole day the boat went on its way. Kabirah felt a bit seasick, but she was also worried because as yet she had not even set eyes on the man whom she assumed had responded to her gestures with the handkerchief. Just for a moment she panicked, thinking she might be the victim of a kidnapping organized by some slave-dealer who had been watching her antics and realized her background and her longing to escape from her own city. But then she saw the Sudanese sailor-slave coming back once again and fixing a lamp on the cabin wall to give some light. No sooner had he left than the person whom she had been waving at, the man whose stature and features were well known to her—so much so that she could envision him even in her dreams—came in.

He greeted her by name, then told her that ever since last week he had commissioned someone to find out where her house was and to check on her story. All that had cost him money, but he had assumed that by so doing he would be giving her some relief and her parents too who would be relieved from worrying about her. "Where are you going?"

he asked her. "I'm going to take you in that sack we used to get you out of Azmur," he went on gruffly, "and put you down in the middle of Salé. You'll have to forget forever every single detail about your journey and the people who helped you. Otherwise that sailor whom you've seen will not be committing any crime if he decides to cut out your tongue. No matter where you may think you've found a safe haven, he'll find you. If I were a Muslim like you, I would have asked your father for your hand. But I'm just a Christian lout from Western Andalus, so we're separated by a religious chasm. I have to admit though that, after thirty years of life at sea, I no longer find such differentiations very significant. Now tell me, where are you going?"

Kabirah was surprised and scared by what she had just heard. This decent man clearly wanted to do the right thing by her, and yet he had a mercurial temperament and clearly would not hesitate to be rid of her. He clearly was not the savior that she had envisaged so readily. A happy deliverance from her troubles would never come as easily as this. She remained silent and was on the point of kissing his hand in gratitude when he used his powerful hand to push her back to her place. It was the first foreign hand that had ever touched her, but it was not to embrace her as she had imagined but instead to push her backwards. As she resumed her sitting position, her expression hardened and disappointment got the better of her. He stood there watching as she burst into tears. After a while he left and closed the door behind him.

At this point she heard some guffaws and cackles from a group of men nearby, but she could not tell if the captain was one of them. Suppressing all negative thoughts, she simply sat there downcast while the boat made its way through the waves towards Salé. She had no idea of how to respond to this man who had smuggled her away. Before long a whole series of other questions began to prey on her: Should she be begging him to help her in some specific way? Once she had disembarked in Salé, would she forget him and his boat forever? Whom could she turn to for shelter? Had he raised the subject of marriage so glibly only in order to remove it for ever from the dream world such as the one that had led her to embark on this particular adventure in the first place? Was he so respectable as to ask her to keep wearing the woolen coat so as to protect herself against the cold at sea? Would the woman who had helped her run away spread the story all around the city of Azmur? Did that mean that her father would pursue the captain all the way to Salé and start searching for his daughter there?

At about midnight she fell asleep. By the time she woke up it was already noontime, and the humidity was stifling her. At her feet she found that someone had left her some breakfast, so, after completing her ritual washing, she ate some of it. The captain came back and stood in front of her; this was the first time that she had set eyes on him close up and in broad daylight. Such was the palpable masculinity of the man that her resolve crumbled and she felt herself wilting as he once again asked her the same question as the day before: When they reached Salé, where would she be going? Even though faced with such crushing indifference, she managed to get a grip on herself. "Do with me what you will," she replied. When he heard that, the man turned away. "Keep your father's coat on," he said. "The wind is going to get much stronger."

When the boat reached the port of Salé, it did not enter the harbor but anchored by the north shore of the estuary. The sailors lowered a small rowing-boat. The Sudanese slave then came over to Kabirah, opened the very same sack, and put her in it; this time he left a slit open so that she could breathe more easily. He then lifted it up by the side where her legs were and lowered her down to another sailor in the rowing-boat. They rowed her ashore and the second sailor rowed back to the boat. Meanwhile the same slave carried her all the way to a house occupied by an old woman who was in the process of lighting a lamp and cooking some oatmeal for supper over a stove. The slave whispered something to the old woman, lowered the sack, and lifted it off Kabirah;

then he left. Kabirah assumed that this woman was either a servant of the captain or else a trustworthy person with whom he could leave such a charge until such time as he could return himself. However, the woman surprised Kabirah by mouthing expressions of sorrow and regret; she did not ask either where she had come from or where she was going. All she said that she was living in the cemetery by the sea-wall of the city and Kabirah could stay with her till morning when the city gates would be opened. In fact, the captain had given her a whole dirham for putting her up for the night.

Kabirah now realized that the one thing she had never thought of had actually come to pass. Now that she had finally met a man to whom she could express the most passionate sentiments that life affords, here he was abandoning her in a cemetery and cutting all ties that might link him to her. Tomorrow she would be swallowed up by a city teeming with men who would not be anything like as gentle as this captain, fearing neither God nor the law; nor would they possess his self-control in understanding her signals and showing restraint when faced with her beauty—especially if she said: Do with me what you will. No sooner had she realized her plight than her entire body was wracked by a fit of shivering, followed by a cold sweat. She felt her body had turned to wood. This transformation became the only kind of revenge that she could take: she would rid herself of the skin of a woman who would both give and take and replace it with that of a dry, mummified skeleton, devoid of all giving. In that way neither rape nor purchase could inflict that much harm on her.

CHAPTER TWENTY-NINE

RAQUSH

Raqush was a pretty girl who grew up in one of the large villages to the East of Tamisna; it was a fertile region, known for the chivalry and bodily strength of its people, men and women alike. Her father owned no land for himself, but worked as a hired farm-hand. He was very proud of his children who played a large role in bolstering his reputation, so much so that land-owners used to ask him for help making their farms productive. His sons and daughters helped him in that endeavor. Actually it rarely happened that the men alone would undertake to do the plowing and gather in the harvest; the women would join in too, and beyond that would tend to household chores, rearing children, and performing other tasks such as pulling up harmful weeds.

From early childhood Raqush used to participate in all the activities that made her father such a renowned farmer. She was skilled at riding all kinds of animals: donkeys for carrying manure and anything planted or harvested in the fields; mules, uncontrollable for anyone else, would be pliant and obedient with her; and horses that she would ride like the wind, so much so that even horsemen would regard her as something proverbial. She used to ride them bareback with no saddle and had no need of spurs to goad or hurt them. Every kind of horse would submit specifically to her control. Even bulls which in springtime would go into a frenzy of rutting at the mere sound of a bird would obey Raqush and follow any shout or gesture she gave.

Right from childhood Raqush had no need of someone to lift her up onto the back of a horse, mule, or donkey. She would not go looking for a high spot from which she could jump on; all that was needed was for her to take a running jump, and there she would be astride her mount leading it by its neck with no need for a bridle.

As Raqush grew up, she became the pivotal factor in her father's household, organizing and arranging everything. Neither her father nor her elder brothers undertook anything on their own, except through negotiations with the landowners immediately before plowing-season. As she grew older, everyone was afraid she would get married; that would mean that the house would become a virtual wasteland in that a vital force that controlled the movements of others, scheduled work assignments, kept an eye on household finances, and above all looked after all kinds of animals would be taken away. Girls like Raqush were regularly snatched up by mothers in search of wives for their sons even before they reached puberty, all as a means of bringing profit to the family and increasing its efficiency and financial situation.

Raqush was two years past puberty when one of the tribal elders who used to assign lands to Raqush's father for plowing asked for her hand for one of his sons. This engagement brought prestige to both sides: after all the girl was renowned for her skills and her blooming health; and no one could fault the tribal elder for stooping to ask for a sharecropper's daughter for his son since it would be profitable for him as well, particularly in his latter years.

Preparations for the wedding in all its finery occupied the fall. Large sums of money were spent outfitting the bride, not to mention the members of both houses and their relatives, as well as replenishing the supplies of linens and crockery, and bringing in supplies of cattle and sheep for slaughter, flour and different types of hors d'oeuvres. All this was aimed at impressing the tribal chiefs, all of whom knew each other and regularly flaunted their wealth and possessions at the major market.

As the wedding day approached, Raqush's family became more and more morose, most especially her mother. There was something they knew, but no one talked about. It was almost as though they were all waiting for the Day of Judgment to arrive. Raqush, a girl who personified chastity and innocence in every conceivable way, would have to be examined according to that utterly trivial measure imposed by tradition, a procedure of enormous importance and one in which an entire life of chastity was encapsulated. Such was its significance that any imperfection detected could be the cause of disasters and terrible consequences which might well involve public exposure, demands for the repayment of expenses, and the besmirching of the honor of both the girl and her family. Ever since the marriage agreement had been reached, the family of the groom had treated the bride's family very discourteously in accordance with custom. Old and young alike had adopted an antagonistic posture, and the final manifestation of such behavior had been the arrival of the party to take the bride to the groom's house; their manners and conversation had been crude enough to make you believe they were going off to war.

The bride arrived, but within minutes the groom's family had declared that she was not worthy to be taken into their care and protection. The remainder of the celebration fell flat. The whole thing came as a complete surprise to everyone, including Raqush. She could not comprehend how it had all happened this way and how it might not have been allowed to happen.

All she had ever wanted to do was to ride horses and please her own father by serving him well. Had she kept doing that for the rest of her life, she would never have felt the need for anything else in order to be completely happy. But who would believe her now, and who could stop tongues wagging and making up nasty stories about her behavior?

A few days later Raqush returned to her mother's house. No one asked her to help them. Her father would not even look at her and her mother was crying so much that she kept looking for somewhere to hide from her daughter so that she could shed her tears alone. Her sisters gave her contemptuous looks and no longer shared anything with her, whether public or private. Everything around her had collapsed, although in herself she knew full well that she had done nothing wrong and had not disobeyed the laws of any God.

One night her father went out with his sons to the market. Once they had left, her mother and the daughters went to bed. Raqush slunk out of the house, got on a horse, and headed north till she reached the river. She then turned towards the shore and kept riding; she was equally expert at horse-riding and staying out of the way of other travelers on the road. Two days later she reached the walls of Salé. She let the horse loose and abandoned it, and then entered the village underneath the wall. Thereafter she decided not to hold back or be afraid of anything in the course of earning a living, any kind of living, now that she was separated from her family by a wave as lofty as mountains.

CHAPTER THIRTY

MAMASS

When Mamass was a young girl, her family finally settled
in the town of Tafilalet on the road from Salé to Meknes after
a long period during which they had lived as itinerant land-
laborers, something they had inherited from their ancestors.
In their encampment they used to receive visits from one of
the Sultan's guards, who served as a protector of roads; he
had been connected to their family when they had worked as
laborers in Wadi Malwiyah in the high mountains. He spoke
the same language as they did, and had memorized the same
festive songs and poetry in praise of their ancestors, something that stirred their emotions to the core.

At first he visited them once every month, but then it
became every Thursday night. He used to spend the entire
evening in their company, singing songs to the accompani-
ment of tambourines and flutes. The male voices of father,
son, and visitor would be matched and rivaled by mother,

daughter, and younger sister with their softer feminine tones. They would sing of chivalry, tenderness, and longing all at once, and in the thrill of the moment the two young people were allowed to give free expression to their sentiments. Mamass's father would repeat the refrains to these poems, almost as though poetry provided a kind of liberated and sacrosanct arena in which there was no moral arbiter and the overriding authority of custom and modesty held no sway.

It was only a few months before this road-guard was coming to the encampment every day and staying over night, bringing food supplies with him just as though he were a member of the family. Without any ceremony performed or witnesses summoned the guard came to regard the house as his own and Mamass as his wife. Her own family accepted the scenario without any objection or question, a kind of tacit acknowledgement of a situation on which they had not been consulted on the day when it had actually come into effect. It may well have been the case that Mamass and her "husband" did not think about the situation either or bear in mind the particulars and complexities involved. That at any rate was the way the parents understood things, and that is the way it was. With that in mind, what point was there in arguing over something when there was a danger of it getting totally out of hand?

There was nothing odd or irregular about this mode of conduct among these migrant workers. Marriage contracts were not regarded as binding, and in any case it was rare to find people qualified to draw them up at markets and festivals. The overseers of religious practice did not bind them rigidly to religious dogma out of consideration for their situation; women would regularly be exchanged at random festive occasions and holidays. For such folk loyalty was a virtue exalted by memory and qualified by its particular yardstick. When relationships broke up, the event was neither preceded by angry scenes nor followed by feelings of failure and loss.

Once it was clear that Mamass was expecting a child, her father decided to take her to visit the shrine of Shaykh Abu Ya`zi in Taghia. They were accompanied by Mamass's "husband" who had obtained permission from the commander of the road-guards. This was a journey blessed from every point of view.

A son was born and was named Amnay, meaning "cavalier." He was not even one year old when orders were issued transferring the boy's father to duties guarding the roads close to Tazah. Three months later he came back to the encampment to see his wife and son and told them that his circumstances were such that he could not take them back to live with him. Rumor had it that the father's unit was about to be divided into two, with one half of it going to guard the roads by Sijilmasah. The guard left the town of Tafilalet, and Mamass walked behind him carrying the boy on her back. She followed him for a long way, and but only decided to turn back when she noticed he was no longer even bothering to turn round and look at her. She threw some rocks at him, then collapsed on the ground, with the little boy crying on top of her. This separation was actually divorce.

After less than a year Mamass was married to a man much older than her. She loathed him and totally rejected him. Thereafter she was married a number of times, over ten in fact, but she never rediscovered that magic that she had found with the man who had given her Amnay. Her last husband was a man ten years younger than her, and she decided to stay with him since he could sing well and shared many of her tastes. But there came the day when he hit her son, Amnay, who, at the age of ten, was typically brash and obstinate. Mamass was furious and decided to break up with this man as soon as possible. It was the time of year immediately before the Great Feast when the people of Tafilalet take their sheep to Salé for the people of that town and others in the region to slaughter at feast-time. Mamass insisted on accompanying her husband to keep an eye on the flock and help the family on market days in Salé. On the second day of the bedlam that accompanied the selling of the sacrificial animals, Mamass slunk away from her husband's family's tent and headed for the part of the market where other items were on sale. She asked some of the old women who were selling tooth-cleaners what was the best way to the closest city-gate, then went on her way and entered a strange new world she had heard about but never seen. As life in the city swallowed her up, she insisted on one thing to the exclusion of everything else relating to her personal circumstance: that no man would ever become so familiar with her that he would feel himself empowered to strike her son, Amnay. He was the very pulse that served as a measure of her own life; he constituted the priceless memory of the man who had abandoned her. She had loved him dearly, and no man had ever managed to make her feel as happy as he had done. She was ready to sell anything just so long as she could buy things for Amnay that would suit his impudent and intemperate behavior. Her dream was that, when he reached adulthood, he would manage to achieve a rank that would allow him to exert authority over other men.

CHAPTER THIRTY-ONE

No one in the city of Salé seemed bothered about these women's stories nor the general welfare of the other people who were living in a set of warehouses that had long since lost their commercial prestige and now simply housed indigents and social outcasts, not to mention the filthy streets where the women's neighbors were certainly not the kind of people with the influence to have the women ejected from their quarters. There was no point in having people in the city know about these women's stories in any case, since it would not have changed anyone's mind about them, altered the brutally unfair opinions that everyone had about them, or lessened the citizens' anxieties about the presence of such women in their midst. These were women of ill repute and were ignored; even people who normally made a show of charity were cagey about them. If the Governor had permitted it, they would have set up a communal stake where they could burn the women to a cinder; there would have been a seething crowd, with paeans of joy yelled forth, teeth bared, nostrils flared, mouths frothing, eyes gleaming, and barbaric instincts purged in the heat of the flames. Beyond all that, had some Salé aristocrat been given the opportunity to take one of the women as a second wife, he would have been quite willing to trade his reputation for it; he would have seen no problem whatsoever in flouting custom that way. After all, the women were all well-versed in the correct, legally sanctioned ways to operate in polite society. There was clearly nothing to stop them serving as counselors to some of the more miserable society dames of Salé.

So it was that Governor Jarmun decided to house a selection of these women in the Oil Hostelry, particularly in the wake of the series of disastrous decisions he had made that had led to the departure of so many merchants from the town. His police chief had told him that the women would be able to afford the rent and pay for protection and other kinds of support. The sums involved would be hardly less than the taxes that the merchants had been paying, and that was the amount that he was supposed to send to the capital in Fez each month; for several months now he had been paying out of his own pocket.

The news spread from the Governor's mansion like wildfire and aroused a great amount of ire in the city. A group of jurisconsults went to visit the Governor, hoping that they could persuade him not to implement his plan regarding the Oil Hostelry. They drew the Governor's attention to the fact that his plan would cause great harm to the city's reputation, since when garbage is collected at a single spot, it smells much worse than if it is dispersed. In any case, the need to send taxes to the capital in Fez did not legitimate the use of charges such as he was intending to impose; that was particularly the case when the charges in question were the result of illicit activities.

Jarmun was worried that this particular group might raise a complaint to the Sultan without his knowing about it, so he stopped renting out the remainder of the rooms in the Hostelry to women of this type, but instead confined himself to appointing a "supervisor" whom the women would have to obey, namely Tudah, along with her agent, Julia, Pedro's daughter. To them he appended the five women from diverse backgrounds mentioned above and six others from a particular tribe that the Governor's forces had compelled to pay the amount of taxes that they owed. Faced with the soldiers, the men of the tribe had run away, leaving the women behind. Jarmun had gone so far as to arrest some of the women, specifically with a view to putting them in the Oil Hostelry.

The Governor charged his aide, a man named Ja`ran, to collect rent and other charges from these women. They soon got used to receiving instructions by way of Tudah, their intermediary, and inuring themselves to the regime imposed on them. Tudah made a specific point of provoking Mamass, she being the mother of the recalcitrant boy, all of which led to a full-scale scrap between the two women. Ja`ran intervened with the doorman, and guards were summoned. Everyone in the Hostelry, with the exception of Shamah, her husband, and Abu Musa, were then summoned to the Governor's mansion. Once there, the boy was taken away and given a good beating by the guards, while his mother, Mamass, was given fifteen lashes as a warning to all the women that they were required to do what Tudah told them.

Within weeks individual rooms and other space in the Hostelry had been occupied by perfumiers, pharmacists, and a variety of bachelors from army and navy. There were even some fortune-tellers and composers of talismans. Once the Hostelry had turned into this new kind of venue, Shamah stopped making her daily visit to the Marshal's house where she would teach his daughters, wives, and other daughters of the nobility a number of skills for a stipend fixed by the Marshal himself. When this happened, the Marshal himself sent her word, insisting that she continue to visit his home in spite of the implied stain on her reputation from living in the Hostelry. In fact, the Marshal seized the opportunity to discuss with her once again his desire to help her find some-where more appropriate to live away from the Hostelry.

When the Marshal insisted, Shamah found herself compelled, such was her awareness of his goodness, to relate to his senior wife her experiences with Abu Musa: how the Governor had schemed one night to have the city gate closed early with her husband outside, had then sent someone to bring her to his residence, and then had a fit of scratching that kept him away from her; and how her husband had spent the night in the cave with Abu Musa and had seen him instigate the scratching that had hit the Governor at exactly the same moment. Shamah explained that, since she had no child of her own as yet, for the time being she wanted to stay in the Hostelry close to this man; as far as the awful things she saw, heard, and smelled every day and night in the Hostelry, they were of no concern to her.

Amnay, Mamass's son, was the instigating factor in a great deal of the fuss that used to happen in the Hostelry. He would spend the majority of his time, early morning and late at night, wandering around the corridors on the different floors. One of his favorite pastimes was to fire off a slingshot that he always kept with him, sending stones flying in all directions. One day he had the idea of aiming a sharp stone at the stork in its nest on top the willow-tree, it being the Hostelry's oldest inhabitant and the senior member of the group to whom generations of pious citizens in Salé had made charitable gifts—the phenomenon for which Salé had become famous in distant cities and cultures with which the commercial community of the city had had contact. This wretched boy aimed a stone at the bird and struck his target fair and square. The stone pierced the bird's stomach, and it plunged to the ground in the middle of the Hostelry, stone dead.

When the news spread abroad, everyone in the Hostelry and city as a whole was grief-stricken. The supervisor of endowments arrived and noted the death. They announced that payment from the endowed funds would be suspended until such time as a successor for the bird took up residence in the nest; the only exception would be those funds that were designated for the care of birds of other species.

For Tudah this presented a golden opportunity to get Ja`ran to inform the Governor that the wretched son of Mamass had killed the stork. Guards arrived, hauled the boy away from his mother, and took him to the Governor's mansion. Mamass followed behind the men, cursing, weeping, and shouting, not caring about anyone or anything. She stayed waiting there outside the prison for two whole nights. When he was released, she checked him over and discovered traces of a severe beating on his backside.

A few days later some people were aroused very early

in the morning by the sound of something heavy falling from the top of the Hostelry into the courtyard. When lamps were lit, it was clear that the thing in question was a woman's corpse. It was Tudah, now dead, with blood streaming from her nose and mouth.

The Hostelry was locked, and everyone except for Shamah, her husband, and Abu Musa were taken away to prison. Some unauthorized persons were discovered inside the Hostelry, their presence only known to Ja`ran and the doorman. Once the Governor had questioned everyone, he let them all go except Mamass, the mother of Amnay, who was suspected of having committed the crime. It was alleged that the police extracted a confession out of her: she had gone into Tudah's room at night where she was sleeping alone, had strangled her, and then thrown her body over the edge of the balcony, and all in order to avenge her son.

No more was ever heard about Mamass or her son. The Governor now charged Tudah's assistant, Julia, Pedro's daughter, with the supervision of the women's affairs.

CHAPTER THIRTY-TWO

`Ali no longer went out every day to accompany Abu Musa to his cave, but Shamah saw no harm in simply leaving him at home while she went out to teach the children in the Marshal's house. When she left, he would either be still asleep or else busy drawing design patterns on strips of wood that he would sell to plasterers to help them in putting up wall decorations. One day while `Ali stayed at home, Shamah went to work in the early afternoon and took with her bathing equipment and a change of clothing. She told him she might stay in the baths till just before sunset. She left the Marshal's house a bit earlier than usual and headed for the large bathhouse near the mosque. She found it closed for repairs for the entire day, and so went straight home, imagining that she would either find `Ali just woken up or else still having a long nap. But `Ali was not in the room, and the door was not locked either. She thought it odd for him not to be there because he had not mentioned anything that might take him away from the room. She took a look round, then went out and came back in again. Taking a look over the balcony at the shops below, she could see no one around at that time of day. Just then she noticed a door partially ajar and the face of one of her female neighbors just visible. It turned out to be Ijja who beckoned her to come down. Forgetting in this moment of concern that she never spoke to these women or went near their rooms, Shamah found herself standing face to face with Ijjah, who, with a gesture of her hand, informed her that her husband was in the room of a woman from his own country.

Shamah could not believe her ears. Had she not been convinced that this wanton woman was lying to her, she would certainly not have rushed to the door of Julia, Pedro's daughter, and discovered `Ali there engaged in a conversation that seemed to be almost over. Shamah staggered backwards, then rushed back upstairs to her own room. Shutting the door behind her, she collapsed on the bed. The noises she made were neither tears nor laughter, neither groans nor complaints; the plain and simple truth was that she had lost control over her feelings and was unable to think straight. All of a sudden she seemed to recover her normal tranquility and equanimity.

"Very well," she told herself, "so be it! The heavens may fall on the earth, but I love him, don't I? Hell itself may emerge from this perfidious woman's navel, but I still love him. Who can love him the way I do? This is the way he repays my love for him? I still love him, do I not? Has he ever once said he would not behave this way? We have throttled him and taken him away from his own mother. Does a woman of his own people have anything else that we've deprived him of all this time? Has he been seeing her before today without my knowing about it? Isn't it reasonable for a human being to make a mistake and then repent? Is this his only time? He can repent then. The real problem is that other people know about it. I am supposed to ask for news about my own broken necklace from a group of women who have never bothered about scandal? So how exactly did she manage to draw `Ali in? Did she tell him about my nocturnal visit to the Governor's house, and he believed her! Yes, that is exactly what the pig-farmer's daughter did in order to entice him. Why on earth didn't he ask me about it himself and find out what had really happened? I could have asked him to forgive me for having kept things from him, and all because of our love for each other and a desire on my part to spare him the agony of doubt. I wonder, was this incident something he wanted, or did it happen unexpectedly as a result of her fiendish machinations? But that's not important. What matters is that he loves me, and she knows nothing about the things that tie the two of us to each other. Poor woman, those men spoiled her innate beauty by raping her! What can happen between two people when the heart of one is broken? What has happened is not important. That woman cannot really love; she just threw dirt in his path. He can wash it all away, and then I can use my own love to restore his heart to its pristine state of purity. Now I can open the door, go looking for him and bring him home as though nothing had happened. I shall surmount any sense of shame or doubt he may feel and not even give him the chance to apologize. I wonder though, will he be sitting outside the door, or is he still where I spotted him? Maybe he has left town and taken the road to the North, just like Pedro who fled when he heard about the fate of his wretched daughter. I know this man and how extremely sensitive he is. Now he's feeling pain in his heart; his breathing is fitful; his very soul is wracked by pain and regret. When a man commits a sin and betrays his own self, where is he supposed to hide? What crime can he have committed to impose itself between him and his own heart? I do not deserve him, it seems. The fault is mine, for insisting that we both live in the midst of this crowd of female reprobates, women who can challenge misery itself with displays of various types of debauchery and surmount their own downfall by claiming that nothing matters and nothing is shameful! I have lived here and have insisted on staying here, all out of a belief in the righteousness of Abu Musa. `Ali is well aware of that, and yet he does not know quite how indebted I myself am to Abu Musa. In fact, does Abu Musa himself even know what has happened now, or what happened before? I don't know. There's no doubt that he can uncover people's secret lives and indeed have a major effect on their way of life. If not, how could he possibly have rescued me from the clutches of the Governor on that particular night? Well, the solution is now in his hand, and he will certainly not refuse me. I will go so far as to tell him exactly what `Ali has done to me after everything that I have done for him. Actually everything that I have done has been for my own sake because I love him just as much as I love my own self. He has endured everything for my sake. But for me, he would never have had to endure the Governor's harassment and the losses in his trade, nor would he have been falsely accused and put in prison. The whole thing would have had no real value if I had not realized quite how far he was aware of the amount of love I was giving him. Could it be that he was simply kidding me; his love was merely a fancy that I had constructed for myself in my quest for a spot in which to place my love and a lyre on whose strings I could play my affections? No, I will not go to see Abu Musa; it is wrong to impose oneself on the sanctuary of the elect or seek them out in order to find answers to one's needs. Had he seen anything that demanded his involvement, he would have done it. Perhaps this incident brings with it some good that at this particular moment I cannot understand. This is all so much nonsense, so why don't I strangle Pedro's daughter and hurl her from the topmost corridor of the Hostelry just as the other woman did earlier on? Then I shall be a woman. And yet, why have I waited so long and endured so much merely in order to end up as a normal woman, wracked by jealousy and prepared to kill for it? If I were to do such a thing, I would provide fate with a course of action that afforded no protection; the Governor would achieve his dearest wish by putting me in prison or else adding me to his personal harem for a while, after which I would be thrown to the dogs. Were I to do so, I would nullify the Sultan's generosity towards me, not to mention the wise counsel of the noblewomen with whom I was raised—Al-Tahirah and Umm al-Hurr. That would be a disaster! If only I could restrain myself and entrust my future to God...if only!"

She felt herself enveloped in a nightmare that made her have doubts about her own fervent belief in the triumph of good. She was overcome by a dark suspicion, almost like noxious weeds about to stifle the roses of magnanimity planted in the generous soil of her heart. "What a scandal," she told herself, "for me to have only ever found pleasure in giving! That's what has laid me open to failure, and now I find myself under torture. I've wasted my innate gifts and squandered everything on a set of hopes that were only aimed at pleasing other people. I've always refused to admit that I'm merely a weak, naïve woman. The realities of life have no time for people with fancies like mine."

Shamah's intention with all these thoughts was to provide some resolution to her current state so that she could re-establish the routine of her own relationship with life. She had the impression that a set of evil forces were operating against her own true nature; by forcing her to retire into her own interior wilderness they hoped to put a stop to all further acts of giving. She was anxious to console herself with the fact that she had been unlucky. Her situation was no different from that of many other people. Even supposing there were people deserving her gifts, she might well have differences with them from the very first encounter. She now started blaming herself all over again for the way she had come to regard herself as someone totally engaged with other people. She began to question the extent to which she had properly estimated the real capacities of that one person to whom she believed herself to have given so much without cost or consideration. She could recall so easily various attitudes that had shaped her life with `Ali; only now, viewing things in perspective, did she realize that, in her frenzied desire to liberate him from the demands of time and space she had only succeeded in strangling the man. In essence he was just a poor, simple man, one of those people who is content to fill his life-vessel with a single drop of water, while she had wanted him to drink an entire ocean. In fact all he could manage were tenuous and ephemeral connections whereas she had imagined that the two of them in their passionate fusion were as close as could be, closer that that type of mystical fusion that Al-Shustari* describes in a poem which she had memorized from her former mistress, Al-Tahirah.

Thoughts like these kept racing through Shamah's mind, like fire catching chaff. After a while she managed to get a grip on herself, just as she had been brought up to do. "God forbid!" she told herself. "I'm feeling insanely jealous, and that has cruelly exposed my pretensions to always being the giver. Actually it's sheer egotism. The truth of the matter is that I was the one doing the taking, otherwise why this crushing jealousy now?"

She rolled over on the bed, then rolled back again. She stood up in alarm and started pacing back and forth, but then fell back on the bed again. At first she managed to stifle her tears, but before long she burst into loud sobs. She kept thinking of her mother and started complaining about her lot as though she were standing right there in front of her. For a while she felt incredibly weak and psychologically depressed, but then she calmed down, stood up again, opened the door and breathed in some of the air wafting upwards from the Hostelry below, full of the scent of spices and henna. Just then she had the sudden sensation that an entire century had

Al-Shustari: a renowned mystical poet of Andalusian origin.

gone by since she spotted her husband down below.

Time for evening prayer came, and `Ali returned. Had she even looked up at him, she would have noticed that he had visited the baths before going to the mosque. But she didn't look up either then or in the days to come; she didn't look at him nor did she make it possible for him to look at her either. She neither spoke to him nor gave him the opportunity to talk. Even so, her expression showed no sign of anger or resentment, nor did any of her gestures suggest that she was bottling up intense feelings. To the contrary, all was serene and submissive.

For his part `Ali realized that he had done wrong and felt that Shamah was watching his every move and gesture. He didn't dare talk about anything. He dearly wanted to cry in front of her, but he didn't. He wanted to bow before her and beg her to forgive him, but he didn't. Even though he continued his normal routine, it was as though he were being crucified. He cherished the thought that time would be able to heal what had been spoiled, but at the same time he was nagged by the thought that merely repairing what had been spoiled would not be the whole story. During the period of time he had spent so close to her, studying her moral up-bringing, his own intuition had been enhanced, and he was abundantly aware of the sheer force of her personality. All that made him suspect that things had indeed fallen apart. The part of her that still remained was much, much less than it had been before.

`Ali went to look for Abu Musa because he wanted to accompany him to his cave by the sea, but he could find no trace of him. All of which served to confirm his fears that it was actually Shamah who had been accompanying Abu Musa—at least in spirit—to the cave by the sea, and all in order to cast her vision towards the distant horizon after turning her back on him and thus on present and past combined.

CHAPTER THIRTY-THREE

A little over a month passed after this incident. Shamah kept waiting for her own internal equilibrium to be restored to its normal state, so that she in turn could help `Ali feel better and rediscover either his former state of mind or even some other relationship with her. But then news spread throughout the Hostelry that Julia, Pedro's daughter, was gravely ill. The doctor whom the Governor had ordered to visit the Hostelry monthly and examine the women ordered that Julia be moved to the lepers' colony outside the walls. She did not actually have leprosy, but the onset of the disease was evident in the red blotches on her skin which would eventually kill her and infect any partner by contagion. People said that Julia had known about her illness for years, but never told anyone. A number of foreign men had come down with the disease after entering this Hostelry.

When `Ali heard the news and understood the implications of what people were saying, he realized that at long last a hand from on high had intervened to put an end to his happiness with Shamah; perhaps it was because he really was not worthy of her. He had always felt at a loss in the face of her infinite ability, like some piece of straw in a vast expanse of space. Now this dreadful calamity had arrived to put an end to their married life. All that remained was for him to end it all. So one morning he left the city and never returned. People told Shamah that 'Ali had been seen crossing the river to the North of the city with a bag over his shoulder; he was heading North.

"What made him leave?" Shamah asked herself, her nerves in shreds. "What on earth made him leave? He should have stayed. Who could look after him as well as I can? What was he ashamed of? Aren't we living in this Hostelry of vice? Don't we witness every day extraordinary things that are brought upon us by fate? Perhaps he has taken his illness with him back to his birthplace. Now I begin to understand. Pedro's daughter detested the people of this land; that's why she kept company with merchants from Christian territories, and they're the ones who gave her this awful disease. When they left the Hostelry for ever, Julia decided to turn her attention to 'Ali and to bring him down with her. As far as she was concerned, 'Ali was merely one among many infidels in Muslim territory. The fact that he had converted to Islam was of no concern to her.

Why had he now deprived her of the chance to stand over his grave if he was now so sure that he would die just like Julia? Was he so sure that his days on earth were now numbered? Why had he abandoned all hope of a cure? Have we not witnessed together a whole series of miraculous events? Isn't Abu Musa, our neighbor in this Hostelry, someone with connections to the world of wonders and miracles? Do you assume that his faith would be unable to cope with such imagined power? So why on earth did he leave? Why?"

Inside her Shamah now felt a void as profound as the abyss of silence and limitless expanse of time itself. The space around her was a wilderness with thousands of wild beasts circling around; the unforeseeable future was full of foreboding. After everything that had happened, what amazing feat could she pull off now? She really needed a safe haven; she needed love. At this point the figure of her former mistress, Al-Tahirah, Judge Ibn al-Hafid's wife, appeared to her. There she would be, sitting on a lofty seat. From that position, robed in her garments of pious devotion, she would patiently dispense her loving care to other people. Now Shamah's dearest wish was to be able to adopt the very posture in which she had watched her mistress of old. She remembered in particular the day when Al-Tahirah's husband, Ibn al-Hafid, had decided to marry a second wife. Al-Tahirah had neither gone to pieces nor flown into a rage; to the contrary, she had simply detached herself from certain things, almost as though she felt she herself had enough already and could thus dispense with them altogether. She felt obliged to keep on giving of herself and to shine brightly till the day she died.

So Shamah did indeed adopt her former mistress's posture. As the days went by, she managed to find contentment and to surmount her former problems. There were just two new aspects to her life: firstly, every afternoon the Marshal sent a maid from his own household to stay the night in the Hostelry with Shamah and then return to the house next morning; and secondly, Abu Musa was very solicitous about her well-being. Two or three times a week he used to come and knock on Shamah's door. When she opened the peephole, he would greet her and she would respond. He would then give her a smile and depart. He had never behaved this way before, and as far as Shamah was concerned, this new level of concern for her was a sure indication of the fact that this man knew everything. He knew that he was the reason for her decision to stay in the midst of a raging fire in this vice-ridden Hostelry; he knew what had happened to `Ali; he knew that, now she was reconciled to a loss of all her hopes, she would no longer be expecting anything. But at least she was content, that in fact may have been why he was so concerned about her. What a kind man he was! What a kind man! But what a cruel man too!

Shamah was now convinced that, ever since she could remember and long before she had ever met Abu Musa, her own fate had been determined by his actions. He was her guardian angel. She was still not sure why on her excursion to the Eastern regions she had been accompanied by a palace-woman who acted like some kind of guardian without making her aware of the fact. By now she could say for certain that her divorce from Al-Jawra'i had been engineered within the palace itself so that she could become part of the Sultan's own harem; Jarmun the Governor had written to the Chief of Police in the capital city of Fez describing Shamah's unique charms. As preparation for the divorce Al-Jawra'i had been criticized for his marriage to Shamah in the intimate circles of the Sultan's court. That is why Al-Jawra'i had told her to beware of wolves. When he had told her about the plans for the expedition to the Eastern regions, he had called her by her own name of Shamah; he must have been convinced that the dream he had developed for a life with a woman called "Warqa'" was about to come to an end. Perhaps this exercise in authority could be regarded as some kind of restitution, in that the police authorities had claimed that Al-Jawra'i was not fulfilling all his conjugal duties towards his wife. However the judicial separation had been so timed to occur after the conquest, the defeat of those tribes which had led to the mobilization of such a huge army. Shamah herself had witnessed the movements of this enormous force of men for two days and nights in Tazah. She had heard the clash of armor and the rousing choruses; she had wondered at the thousands of pack-animals and hundreds of muezzins calling the faithful to prayer. Could it be, Shamah wondered, that she was one of the prizes that had been transported along with the expedition so that the prospect of her forthcoming marriage to the Sultan could increase the pleasure of victory? Could the Sultan and his huge army have been defeated so that he would leave her alone and go away, while she would be protected against the kind of rapine and aggression that he could expect? Was it the shipwreck of the entire fleet that had put an end to their entire plan? No, no, it was sheer exaggeration and egotism to suggest that the loss of a king and her own rescue from capture were somehow linked. But no, this was no exaggeration! Was it not the same thing whether a single woman was captured or a whole host of people? So let twenty fleets founder, as long as Shamah's honor was protected.

Shamah had the impression that the city of Salé was going through the same period of trauma as she was; it was feeling the same pains. She may even have imagined that she had come to encapsulate the city as a whole or that both of them were sharing the same portion of divine justice. However there was a difference: while Shamah sought to escape her trials by lifting herself up, the city of Salé lay on its stomach and groveled. Ever since the merchants had left, all prosperity had vanished. The city's wounds deepened and festered as day followed day. Everything was topsy-turvy.

CHAPTER THIRTY-FOUR

A whole winter passed with no rain. By the end of summer the Governor had ordered the owners of grain silos to open up their stores, but they raised their prices. Pedro's daughter, Julia, died in the fall; the illness had taken control so that the extremities of her body turned putrid. People refused to allow her to be buried in the Muslim graveyard, and the Judge and Governor were both afraid of trouble if they disregarded such sentiments. In addition people were worried that, if Julia's body were simply left in its coffin by the wall of the lepers' quarters, the body would putrefy even more. Shamah went to see the Marshal concerning the possibility of Pedro's daughter being buried in the Muslim graveyard, and he collected a number of witness statements to the effect that, based on her behavior, she had died a Muslim. With that, she was buried in the Muslim graveyard and that was the end of the matter.

There now followed an entire year of drought in Salé and many other parts of the country as well. In the fall of the following year a few clouds put in an appearance, but they were rapidly dissipated by gale force winds that destroyed a number of trees. People became fed up with staring at a blue sky day after day. All the wells dried up, and supplies in the cisterns quickly ran out. The springs that would water Salé's gardens and operate the water-mills to grow crops, fruit, and flowers all went dry. No one knew for sure whether there was enough grain left in the silos, while the pasturage in a number of neighboring forests dried out and, as a result, fires would frequently break out in the brush. There was so little fodder that animals became visibly thinner; many sheep were slaughtered without replenishing the supply. Cows' udders dried up too, and there was no flesh on their flanks. Donkeys and mules could no longer be loaded or ridden; they would spend the steaming-hot days rolling in paddocks and kicking up dust, suffering all the while from the bites of huge, noxious flies. Large numbers of dogs, with no flocks of sheep to guard, came into the cities looking for corpses by the walls, so much so that people began to worry in case they started digging up corpses from graves. Birds would hover for a long time before finding a leafy branch on which to perch or an insect that was prepared to risk venturing outside its hole.

By the beginning of the third consecutive year of drought, shortage of food and high prices made the situation very grave. Bread could simply not be bought, even for a whole cluster of gold jewelry. Governor Jarmun accused certain people of sitting on stores of grain, but upon examination they were found to have nothing. People kept expecting a camel caravan to arrive, with grain that some Salé merchants had purchased from Christians who had brought it over to Tangier. But the caravan never arrived because Bedouin bandits attacked it, killed the guards, and made off with the grain.

Jewelry and household furniture was sold off cheap, and lands and estates as well. Lights were no longer lit at night because people kept whatever oil was left as food. People ate bran, bean-pods, maize-husks, lotus-fruit pits, and carob seeds. Rumor had it that a guest who came to the Oil Hostelry brought with him a handful of olive-oil pulp, the residue after it had been squeezed. Roots from certain plants would be pulled up, dried, ground, and then eaten dry.

From this pulp the women in the Hostelry used to extract whatever oil they could so that they could prepare the best possible meal in the starving city. From the time when the famine had started to turn grave, Abu Musa had been bringing each woman two fish every week and putting them by her door; it was almost as though he had undertaken to look after his women neighbors and realized that they were more prone to disaster than the other women in the city.

Beyond that he had been providing them each month with a supply of wild-root flour which was good for making the most wholesome and delicious bread.

Up till now Shamah was the only one who had shared Abu Musa's spiritual company and acknowledged the secret that no one else knew—that secret that Shamah had decided to reveal to `Ali one day if only he had not decided to leave, namely how she had managed to escape from Jarmun's sinister scheme. But now all Abu Musa's women neighbors were beneficiaries of his favors; they kept asking themselves how it was possible for this one man to provide so much for them when all the other men in the city, far more robust than he, kept on complaining of hunger. They could not understand how he could go out of the city alone and take pathways that were now off limits even to patrols carrying arms. What was important was that, after so many years when they had simply ignored him, their attention was now fully focused on him; now they realized that he was one of those really rare men of genuine sanctity, and they of all people knew how valuable and rare such men were. Ever since each one of them had realized the fate that had brought them to this particular Hostelry, she had come to the clear conclusion that there were no pious people left on earth, especially men. This man might prove to be an exception. They would go their way and he his, and neither side would bother about the other. Between them and him was the same space as between earth and sky. What seemed ironic was that the lack of rain and the onset of drought as the heavens turned their back on the earth was the thing that had made the women wake up to their neighbor Abu Musa. It was hardship that had brought them closer together. As for now, how very close they all were to his lofty station, and how enormous their sense of shame as they saw him every day!

All sense of security vanished, and every road was considered dangerous. People inside the city no longer visited their garden properties outside the walls; things went so far that pilgrims to Mecca, men and women, were robbed and came home barefoot, naked, and starving. During the third winter season since the rain had stopped falling even worse things happened. People started eating corpses and human flesh, even young children. Everyone was well aware that this was happening and turned a blind eye, but Jarmun sent his troops to arrest a woman who was said by her neighbors to have eaten a child; people were instructed to gather for a public stoning, and she was stoned to death. The veil of chivalry fell from the faces of any number of people who were noted for their pious devotion. The Marshal of the Sharifs himself, in spite of the august nature of his position, could not stop himself spitting in the face of a midwife who came to see him thinking that she could reveal to him some scandalous information about a servant girl who had formerly been one of his favorites but had now given birth to a child. People's conversations were full of insults and crudities; all sense of civility and respect between parents and children, old and young, common folk and the elite, seemed to have vanished.

Now the plague arrived in certain quarters and assumed grave proportions; some quarters were completed emptied of inhabitants. People were being buried with neither shroud nor prayers. It was said that most people perished in those quarters where some folk were alleged to have eaten rats. Some people tried to flee to other countries, but fear, murder, and robbery stopped them in their tracks, not to mention the dire rumors to the effect that the famine was widespread.

On more than one occasion during this third winter the heavens had a hearty laugh by thundering loudly. Clouds gathered, but to no good effect. On several other occasions the heavens glowered down with a heavy smog which seemed to promise much, and yet all it produced was a few drops mingled with a heavy black dust. Such false hopes made everyone realize that they were being gradually worn down, cursed, and mocked.

CHAPTER THIRTY-FIVE

Ever since the drought had started, people had been going outside the city of Salé to perform the prayer for rain. Their efforts all came to nothing, in spite of the fact that some of the Imams who were summoned to lead the prayers were renowned for their piety. People flocked to mosques in untypical numbers, and food was brought in as alms. Preachers took turns to deliver sermons from the pulpit, and every one of them explained the dire calamity that had befallen the community in terms of the way in which God's servants were disobeying his injunctions. One Friday, the head of the scholars' assembly broke his normal custom by delivering a sermon in which he attributed the lack of rainfall to the large number of reprehensible actions that had been taking place.

That very same afternoon the Chief of Police called him in and demanded an explanation as to precisely what he meant by "large number of reprehensible actions." Was he referring to the taxes that the Sultan enjoined them to pay; or was he perhaps talking about the Governor's beneficence towards a group of poor helpless widows whom he had housed in the Oil Hostelry as an act of charity and mercy and as a way of keeping the Hostelry occupied until such time as the merchants came back; or was he thinking of the Sultan's Governor's determination to deal firmly with all deviants, reprobates, hypocrites and subversives?

The reverend shaykh informed the Chief of Police that he had intended none of these things. When this reply reached the Governor's ears, he gave orders that a decree should be written in the shaykh's name that would be read out in all mosques, one that would reflect his unequivocal views in the following terms:

Of all the reprehensible acts that are at the root of the current disastrous situation, including the lack of rainfall, the direst is the effrontery that people are displaying towards their rulers and the way they continue to defy their rulers' orders, commit offenses that have been explicitly forbidden, and fail to offer assistance to their rulers as they perform their sacred functions.

The Governor was not content merely to have this decree promulgated, but gave further instructions that, when people went out of the city to perform the prayer for rain, their Imam should be none other than the reverend shaykh in person, in that he had not fulfilled that function thus far. So everyone went out of the Sabtah Gate on the sea-side of the city and performed the rain prayer as the Governor had ordered. The Imam for the ceremony was indeed the reverend shaykh. But no rain fell. In fact, a fierce wind blew up depositing frogs and stones on everyone. In response to that the Governor now ordered the shaykh to stay at home and not deliver any more sermons.

The Governor behaved in exactly the same way with a number of preachers and men of religion, until he had managed to silence them all. The crisis went from bad to worse; people were going crazy, not knowing where to turn. It was at this point that one of the Governor's nastier confidants suggested that he should not let slip this golden opportunity to bring down someone who was always opposing him behind his back and was a fierce rival for people's respect, something that was really due only to someone of the Governor's status, namely Abu Musa, the obscure individual who lived in the Oil Hostelry. "If he is such a noble personage," this confidant suggested in conclusion, "then let him show it by ridding people of this crisis; if not, then he should be expelled from the city."

The Governor now sent word to Abu Musa, ordering him to serve as Imam for the rain prayers on the coming

Friday. The people of Salé had different responses to this command: some regarded the whole thing as a joke, while others declared it lamentable, the kind of dreadful decision that was so typical of this particular Governor. Still others suggested that, if this was really a good thing for Abu Musa to be doing, then there would surely be a positive response with him leading the prayers. Abu Musa himself did not respond in any way when he was told of the Governor's order. He carried on with his normal routine, spending the day in his cave beside the sea and eating seaweed. But when he failed to appear at the appointed sunset hour on Friday, the Governor ordered that he be arrested and imprisoned.

The news made Shamah cry. When the Marshal of Sharifs and some city notables heard that Abu Musa had been put in prison, they immediately went to the Governor to get him released. The Governor agreed, but only on condition that Abu Musa not defy his order to lead the rain prayers. He clearly owed this favor to the people in the city who believed him to be a miracle-worker and a devout man of God.

The intercessors went to see Abu Musa in his cell and explained what he needed to do in order to comply with the Governor's orders. He signaled his acceptance and smiled. They then went back and informed the Governor; as a result Abu Musa was allowed to return to the Hostelry at the end of the day. However next day when he tried to leave the city to spend the day in his cave by the sea, the guards at the north gate, acting on orders from the Governor, prevented him from leaving until Friday had passed, that being the day when he would be leading the people in prayer.

CHAPTER THIRTY-SIX

On Thursday morning Abu Musa knocked on Shamah's door. She came out and found him looking resplendent in a costly white jubbah* covered in a white cape; on his head he was wearing a green turban and he was holding a staff. As he stood there in front of her, she noticed his gentle eyes and the radiant look on his face, something that no one had ever seen before because he always went around with his head lowered. "My lady," he said, "come out with me so we can ask God for rain. Tell our neighbors to come out with us."

No one had ever heard this man speak before. However, when Shamah heard him talk, it did not come as a shock because he had long since found a place in her heart. Ever since she had come to live in this Hostelry, she had nursed deep inside her a deep respect for his mission. So how happy she felt today to see him once again caring for her and taking charge of her destiny! Here he was, ordering, or rather asking,

---

Jubbah: a man's outer garment or wrap, often made of heavy material.

her to go outside the city at the Governor's command, the very order that had made her sick to think about ever since she had known him. But she decided to go out with him; if no rain fell, she was quite prepared to follow him to prison. She was well aware that this command was not one he had issued himself; in fact he was doing it against his will. The person who would be conducting the ceremony and leading the prayer would not actually be Abu Musa in person but fate itself. But the agreed upon date for the occasion was Friday, and today was only Thursday. So, if Abu Musa intended to take her and the other women outside the city today, he must have received an order to do so. Everyone would be able to see Abu Musa making his way through the alleys and imploring God for aid, followed by a group of women whom many of them had long since assumed to be possessed by devils. Perhaps his intention was to make fun of them all just as the heavens themselves had done on more than one occasion. If that were the case, then he would go to prison for ever.

All these thoughts went through her mind as she washed herself again and put on her gown and shawl. As soon as she came out, Abu Musa went and banged on the doors of the other women with his staff. They all emerged, either in tears or thunderstruck. Every single one of them assumed that this devout and pure man would never let a day or night pass without invoking curses against them for their behavior, even though they knew that in this period of drought he had kept them supplied with gifts of food. They all stood there unable to speak, just like chickens that have fallen out of their nest. They had no idea what was going to happen.

Shamah emerged in all her finery and Abu Musa put her on his right. Then, with the other women following, he left the Hostelry and headed for another one which was also inhabited by women who had suffered the same fate. He asked them to come out and they did so. People watched in astonishment as this strange procession went on its way; the news spread rapidly and people started talking. They followed behind at a distance, watching to see what would happen. Information soon reached the Governor, and he ordered a group of his spies to keep an eye on things.

Abu Musa and his female entourage left the city by the east gate. This time he was being trailed by a large crowd of men and women, so the gate-keepers could not stop him. In the courtyard of the mosque Abu Musa took off his green turban to reveal a head of disheveled hair. He started intoning supplications which the women would repeat after him. They followed behind as he made a circumabulation, as though there were some kind of pole in the middle of the mosque:

Praise to God Almighty!
O God, take pity on their weakness.
Praise be to God Almighty!
O God, look down upon them.
Praise be to God Almighty!
O God, take pity on their weakness.

His voice rose higher and higher, and the women echoed him. Every one of them burst into tears and wept profusely from tearducts that everyone assumed to have dried up for ever. It was not long before everyone felt the presence of an intense emotional charge. The women were running behind Abu Musa; their feet hardly seemed to touch the ground. Their shoes fell off, and there they all were barefoot. Shawls fell off too, just to show how strong was the trance that had gripped them as part of some kind of cleansing gesture. Their hands were raised to the heavens, and their gaze was such that they seemed to be staring at angels that had descended so far from the heavens that they almost touched the earth. So powerful was the women's trance that it reached out to the thousands of men and women who were watching them from the edge of the mosque. Paeans of praise and alleluias rang out and people starting hugging each other as though they had just been liberated from the chains of hell itself. Nobody knew how or why this thing was happening.

The news spread that Abu Musa and his women neighbors had gone out of the city, but not to pray in the normal fashion, rather to implore God to send rain. Other people went out to the mosque, some who believed what they heard, others who didn't. Some people regarded it as a comic turn, while others thought that the way he had taken his women neighbors out with him was just another instance to add to the pile of insults that fate had poured on the people of Salé. There were those who said that on a day like this even mules would give birth. "Now that all the other men of faith have been dismissed," others pointed out, "this man's the only one we can ask to beg for rain. We've all buried our heads in the sand and despaired of all hope that God might respond to our prayers, so these women are the only people left to lead us." Store-owners closed their shops; men went out of the city, and even cloistered women followed them. By noontime Abu Musa and the women were still performing their circumambulations; his rapture and theirs was becoming yet more intense. He kept intoning the same supplication, while people stared at him from afar. As everyone watched, he was now joined by a group of Sufi devotees, who recited their litanies, stirred their souls, and blended their voices in a single unified

chant that made the entire courtyard vibrate: "Huwwww,"
they repeated in modest transcendent devotion, "huwwww."
Some of them collapsed to the ground and rolled around in
the dust as though begging forgiveness from some monarch.
Some of the people watching were anxious to give them some
water, but the Sufi leaders stopped them. "Don't give them
water," they said. "They're currently sipping the choicest
wines of heaven!" "Leave them to their thirst," said others.
"Eventually the heavens will take pity on all of us who are
thirsty."

With the afternoon call-to-prayer, Abu Musa raised
his right hand and index finger. "Muhammad is the Prophet
of God!" he yelled at the top of his voice so everyone could
hear him. That phrase seemed to be a cryptic conclusion, one
to which the souls of those present could submit. Everyone
stopped as soon as they heard it; people emerged from their
trances, and things fell quiet. The inner circle broke up, and
people rushed forward to embrace Abu Musa, so much so that
he disappeared among the many hands that were trying to
reach for him. People tried to touch him, kiss him, cut off
segments of his clothing, and pull out tufts of his hair. All
the while he stood there enduring the experience valiantly.
Women of the city fell on the Hostelry's women as though
they were angels from God himself; they were all anxious to
acquire one of them as a second wife for their husbands.

After all the hue and cry, everyone returned to the city mosques and then went home, not knowing whether to talk or wait to see what happened.

No sooner had the crowd dispersed than Jarmun proceeded to assemble all his counselors and aides, prime amongst them the Chief of Police. They told him precisely what had occurred and gave him exact details about every house that had taken in one of the Hostelry women as both protection and blessing. They explained that, on explicit instructions from the Chief of Police, the guards had deliberately refrained from inciting the crowd. The point of the exercise had been to avoid providing a golden opportunity for a group of people who for several months had been plotting to gather a mob that could storm and take over the Governor's mansion. Now that the famine had reached crisis proportions, that was what had actually happened in several other cities and tribal regions. Jarmun paid close attention to the advice of his political counselors and religious advisers; he was particularly keen to hear their opinions on the import of Abu Musa's excursion from the city to pray for rain and on the large group of citizens who had followed him.

At this point the Chief of Police spoke up. He described the scene and went on to extol the Governor's decision not to intervene, something that might well have led the crowd to start a riot.

"By God," the Judicial Counselor said, "this is sinful. Women do not go outdoors to pray for rain! Heresy! The whole thing is a blot on our city!"

"Watch your words carefully, revered shaykh," the Chief of Police interrupted sarcastically. "Maybe their prayers will bring us some rain!"

The shaykh had assumed that by expressing his disapproval of Abu Musa's conduct he would earn the Governor's favor. Now he was a bit shaken. "No, no," he retorted. "It's the original act that counts. Even if these women were full of virtue, even if their prayers were to bring us rain, the fact that Abu Musa took them out of the city is still a direct infringement of proper practice. Indeed it is sinful. Even if rain does fall as a result of their intervention, nothing will grow from it, neither crops nor flowers. It will merely fill the mouths of serpents with yet more poison."

At this point one of the Governor's counselors entered the conversation in order to list the infractions that Abu Musa had committed and that would need to be prosecuted, whether or not rain fell: the fact that he had gone out on Thursday, not Friday; that he had taken women out with him instead of men; that a huge crowd had gathered around him, with the direct threat of riot and insurrection, and in contravention of the accepted rituals of prayer.

At the conclusion of this meeting Jarmun issued orders to look for Abu Musa, to keep a watch on his movements, and not to allow him to leave the city till the Governor had decided what to do with him. The police started searching for Abu Musa, but could find no trace of him. None of the women from the Hostelry was in her abode, and no one except the Governor's own spies had any idea where any of them had gone. Shamah had gone to the Marshal's house and had no intention of leaving.

In the dark of night the people of Salé watched as the gleaming stars began to disappear. A West wind blew up, something they had not experienced ever since the drought had started. Rain started to fall, first in drops and then in a deluge; it was careening down. Unable to believe what they were seeing and hearing, they rushed outside to make sure that it really was rain. Leaving their homes, they let their heads and bodies become soaked as the rain streamed down all over them. Knocking on each other's doors, they exchanged blessings and hugs, wept tears of joy, and pondered the meaning of this transcendent moment. "Praise be to God!" they all intoned over and over again, "God still has His secrets on earth. Praise be to Him who has now revealed His secret to us!"

The rain did not let up till the following day. When the time came for Friday prayers, everyone went to the senior preacher who had been confined to his house by the Governor, and brought him out to give the sermon and lead them in prayer. "Hardness of heart is what has kept the rain from us," he said. "Rain is part of God's mercy, and that mercy takes root in people's hearts. But if those hearts are full of false pretenses and egotism, they find themselves blocked and then they turn cruel. There is no room for mercy. Inevitably they must be broken and the vapors of cupidity must dissipate in order for God's judgment to be exercised on them. I find myself among those with broken hearts, just like those women whose supplications were answered yesterday."

When the Governor was told what the preacher had said, he was on the point of having him arrested, because his words ran directly counter to the claims he had made earlier, namely that the reason why rain had stopped falling for so long was because of the sinful behavior of the women. However his own confidants and advisors strongly suggested that at this point he avoid any actions that might cause dissension or a riot. That might well lead in turn to the destruction of his mansion and even his own death.

The Governor kept up his search for Abu Musa and so did his friends. They looked everywhere. People got to hear of this and feared for Abu Musa's life. They too sent people to seek him out. The people who eventually found him were a group of men that the Marshal sent to a particular park. Actually it was Shamah who suggested they look there; she knew that that was where he often took a nap on his way back from the cave by the sea. They found him under a pomegranate tree. At first they thought he was asleep, but soon discovered that he was dead.

CHAPTER THIRTY-SEVEN

Abu Musa's body was carried back to the Grand Mosque for his funeral. People in the city decided to wait till the afternoon prayer to announce the timing so that everyone who wanted to attend could do so. The wings and square of the Grand Mosque were all packed with people praying, and so were the nearby streets. Dozens of reciters made sure that people at the back could hear. The funeral was a muted affair; the only sounds were the tears that trickled from people's eyes and uncontrollable sobs that overwhelmed strong men as well as gentle women. "God be praised," people said, "God be praised! Along with the return of rain has come the sound of tears falling!"

With the prayer-service completed, people once again paid each other visits, exchanged blessings, were reconciled with each other, and wondered at the transcendent miracles that had descended upon them. It was decided that Abu Musa's corpse should be carried to the mosque's cloister; candles should be lit and a dozen muezzins would take turns standing watch over him till morning. When it came time to bury him, two of the groups with the longest standing in the city disagreed: each one wanted him to be buried in its graveyard, claiming that Abu Musa had either been born or had lived on their territory. They decided to postpone the decision till the next day. Both the Marshal of the Sharifs and the senior preacher were agreed that the decision should lie with the person who had been placed at Abu Musa's right hand during the supplications and circumambulation. Everyone was happy with that decision. "Don't bury him in either graveyard," was Shamah's word on the subject. "Bury him in a spot overlooking the sea."

AHMED TOUFIQ: *JARAT ABI MUSA*

An Afterword

Ahmed Toufiq's novel, *Jārāt Abi Mūsā,** originally published in 1997 (2nd ed., 2000) and here translated as *Abu
Musa's Women Neighbors*, participates in a process of novelistic development within its author's native Morocco and the
broader Arabic-speaking world that is, by the very nature of
things, subject to both change and variety.

Several factors, involving both international and local politics,
societal transformations, and cultural influences, have en-
gendered a creative environment for the novelist writing in
Arabic that is as fascinating as it is challenging. The June
War of 1967 and its aftermath demolished any number of

I have indicated the full vocalization of the novel's name on this one occasion
only.

concepts and even organizations that had been fostered and supported by post-independence regimes through the Arab world and led to a wholesale re-examination of the very bases of the Arab sense of identity and the definition of nationhood. The increasing prominence of oil economies, especially in the Gulf region, the isolation of Egypt following its treaty with Israel, the emergence of a vigorous Shi'ite theocracy in Iran, and many local and international conflicts, all these factors played into a vision of the Arab world that was more diffuse, even splintered in form; what Albert Hourani (in his renowned *History of the Arab Peoples*) describes as a "disturbance of spirits."

The novel genre and its practitioners have, needless to say, reflected these trends. Here again, the 1967 June War can serve as a useful divide, between a developmental and imitative phase of the anterior period, crowned by Najib Mahfuz's much celebrated *Trilogy* [1956-57] (a status duly acknowledged three decades later by the Nobel Award in 1988), and a subsequent period in which the now fully "domesticated" genre went in quest of new directions; directions that would be a reflection of a concomitant search for a new and different national and international identity, an awareness of the need to link such a search for identity to both the pan-Arab and local past, and a decision to focus to a greater extent on regional particularities along with all their linguistic, social, and cultural ramifications. In view of what I have just noted about Mahfuz's pioneering role in what may be termed a "first phase," it needs to be emphasized—with due admiration—that a survey of his novels of the past three decades makes it clear that he has joined his younger novelistic colleagues in such a quest. In this context, any number of names might be cited, but for me the most significant would be Jamal al-Ghitani from Egypt, Ilyas Khuri from Lebanon, the late `Abd al-Rahman Munif from Saudi Arabia via Jordan and Syria, and Ibrahim al-Kuni from Libya. The sheer variety of these writers' novelistic output is eloquent testimony to the trends that have just been noted.

Ahmed Toufiq and *Jarat Abi Musa*.

Ahmed Toufiq is currently the Minister of Religious Affairs and Endowments in the Moroccan government. Previous to that he served as Director of the National Library in Rabat, where he also taught at Morocco's greatest institution of higher learning, L'Université de Muhammad V. By training he is a philologist and historian, someone who is fully familiar with the texts—some published, some not—that deal with the pre-modern history of Morocco and its widely variegated regions, the cities of the coast, the great imperial capitals of Fez, Meknes, and Marrakech, and the *"bled as-siba"* (recalcitrant territories, a term retained by the French colonizers of the region) outside the cities and extending into the Amazigh territories of the Atlas mountains. The process of editing and publishing these types of older historical source-text means that Ahmed Toufiq is intimately familiar not merely with the history of his homeland in all its phases but also with the emphases and styles that are characteristic of historical writing about Morocco and its peoples. It is this combination of interests and talents that makes its way into many of the novels that he has written, of which *Jarat Abi Musa* (recently adapted in Morocco as a film) is the most famous.

The interest in this novel starts with the title, which for the translator is itself problematic. In the context of Moroccan society and its deeply entrenched values regarding gender-roles, it begs a number of questions: mostly obviously, of course, who is Abu Musa, but beyond that, how is it possible for a male personage to have contact with a plurality of women in the form of neighbors? Something peculiar and untoward appears to be at work, and thus is the reader drawn into the narrative itself. For the translator into French (and the work has already been published in that language), the task is made much easier by the availability of the specifically feminine form "voisines." However, in order to retain the logic of the original title—one that, to me at least, seems extremely important to the sequence of beginning that is so crucial to the reading of works of fiction, the lack of such gender specificity in English has led me to utilize the title *Abu Musa's Women Neighbors*. I'll confess to having toyed with a variety of alternatives—*Abu Musa and the Women Next Door*, *Abu Musa and His Women Neighbors*, etc., but have thus far settled on the title that introduces this translation.

The first and most obvious question based on the title that I have posed above—who is Abu Musa?—is not to be answered for quite some time, another interesting narrative device of the author. Nor indeed are we to meet the "women neighbors" until almost the end of the novel. Instead we are introduced to the Atlantic-coast port-city of Salé and its grandees (particularly the chief-judge and governor) and its significant role as a commercial center from which a flourishing trade is conducted with Spain to the North and the cities of the Mediterranean—all the way to Genoa and Amalfi. The port is clearly a source of major revenue for the capital city of Fez, several days' journey away in the interior. The relative authority vested in the officials of the two cities and the degree of autocratic power wielded by the evil governor of Salé, Jarmun, are pivotal features of the political scenario within which the novel is set. Right in the middle of this power-game is set the novel's heroine, the stunning blonde beauty, Shamah, of Andalusian origins, lusted after by men and admired by women for her poise and knowledge of the finer points of politesse. Indeed, were it not for the novelist's implied purpose, to illustrate the abuses of power and to show the way in which religion—and especially mysticism—can serve as a cogent force in resisting such undesirable secular tendencies, the novel might well be entitled "the story of Shamah."

Into this narrative of political intrigue, Ahmed Toufiq manages to weave a wealth of detail about court ritual, domestic custom, and not a little history. While the time period is never specifically mentioned, the enormous naval disaster resulting from the Sultan's decision to undertake an expedition to bring his Eastern territories back under control, his narrow escape from death, and his deposition in favor of his son, coincide exactly with the way in which the Marini Sultan, Abu al-Hasan, was replaced by his son, Abu `Inan, in the 14th century CE. The presence of the beautiful Shamah on board the Sultan's vessel (at his request) and the fact that a sinking boat from the fleet is miraculously repaired in midstorm by a mysterious figure who strongly resembles an eccentric figure from Salé, these are part of the fictional magic that Ahmed Toufiq injects into this novel of history whose themes of power and its abuses and the relationship between the secular and the sacred are as much a part of today's Arab world as they were of the pre-modern era so wonderfully depicted in this novel.

Ahmed Toufiq writes his novel in the pellucid style of a philologist and historian who is familiar with the great tradition of pre-modern Arabic prose. In preparing this translation, the major issue for me has been an attempt to reproduce the wealth of information and the precise detail of ceremony and ritual that clearly reflect both his immense erudition and also his desire to produce in novel form a narrative that will appeal to the contemporary reader of Arabic fiction not only in Morocco but also, book distribution permitting, throughout the Arabic-speaking world. That the novel has been converted into film form would suggest that, at least with the former readership, he has achieved that goal.

I should perhaps conclude this "translator's afterward" with something akin to a confession. As a more than occasional translator of Arabic fiction, I find myself no longer attracted by the prospect of transferring to an English readership those works by Arab novelists that will confirm the continuing influence of Western trends in novel writing. As far as the Arabic novel is concerned, we are, as it were, in a post-Nobel award era, and for me the interesting question is to what extent it can contribute to the world novel tradition rather than the reverse. While no one would wish to deny the significance of such trans-cultural influences, I remain in quest of those trends in the Arabic novel that are different and that will impose particular challenges for the Western reader. For me at least, it is in those very unfamiliar voices and the narrative strategies that they invoke—the `Abd al-Rahman Munif of *Al-Nihayat* with which I concluded the first edition of my work on the Arabic novel, and the Ibrahim al-Kuni of *Nazif al-Hajar* with which I concluded the second—that I find the excitement in studying and translating Arabic novels into English. It is in that spirit and that context that I now offer Ahmed Toufiq's *Jarat Abi Musa*.

ROGER ALLEN
November 2004.